MONSTER HIGH

HAUNTED

LITTLE, BROWN BOOKS FOR YOUNG READERS

First published in the United States in 2015 by Little, Brown and Company
First published in Great Britain in 2015 by Little, Brown Books for Young Readers

1 3 5 7 9 10 8 6 4 2

A CIP catalogue record for this book
is available from the British Library.

ISBN 978-0-349-13221-1

Printed and bound in Great Britain by
Clays Ltd, St Ives plc

The paper and board used in this book are
made from wood from responsible sources.

MIX
Paper from
responsible sources
FSC® C104740

Little, Brown Books for Young Readers,
part of Hachette Children's Group
and published by Hodder and Stoughton Limited
338 Euston Road, London NW1 3BH

An Hachette UK Company
www.hachette.co.uk

www.lbkids.co.uk

MONSTER HIGH

HAUNTED

The Junior Novel

ADAPTED BY
Perdita Finn

BASED ON THE SCREENPLAY WRITTEN BY
Keith Wagner

LITTLE, BROWN BOOKS FOR YOUNG READERS
www.lbkids.co.uk

CHAPTER 1

THE GHOSTLY GOSSIP STRIKES AGAIN

A shimmery ghost darted through the undersea ruins of a shipwreck. Bubbles drifted toward the surface of the dark waters. A saber-tooth jellyfish gnawed on a rotting mast. In a shiny flash, the ghost swirled through a crack in the boat's hull and rose up, up, up, bursting with a splash into the air. It was Sirena von Boo—the ghost mermaid.

Cheers rose from Monster High's very own Fear Squad. Music thumped through the stands. Led by Sirena, the diving team was crushing Plankton Prep in the competition!

Sirena zipped along the surface of the pool. Waves of translucent blue hair wafted behind her as she flipped and crested like a dolphin.

"M-O-N-S-T-E-R-S! Monsters! Monsters! Yes, we are!" chanted the Fear Squad.

Sirena touched out at the end of the pool—and disappeared through the concrete. She emerged on deck, looped up into the air, and dove back toward the deep end.

"And once again, thanks to Monster High's aquatic superstar, Sirena von Boo, it looks like the Plankton Prep diving team is all but sunk," enthused the announcer.

Defeated members of the Plankton Prep team sat on the bench with sad expressions on their faces. In the home team stands, Sirena's hybrid friends cheered.

"Go, Sirena!" whinnied Neighthan.

"You go, ghoul!" exclaimed Avea.

"Whooo!" Bonita screamed.

Sirena flew out of the water up to the top of the highest diving board and reached out to give Lagoona Blue a victorious high five.

"Cheers, mate!" The ever-happy Lagoona laughed. With a beautiful twirl, she executed a perfect splashless dive into the pool.

Rochelle the gargoyle was watching longingly from

the sidelines near the locker rooms. If only she didn't sink like a rock whenever she went in the pool.

"Hey, Rochelle," said a shadowy figure beside her. It was Twyla, the daughter of the Boogie Man. Twyla held out her hands to Rochelle for a game of rock, paper, scissors. "One, two, three…" She placed her flat hand playfully over Rochelle's head. "Paper beats rock. I win!"

But Rochelle didn't react. She was watching Sirena and Lagoona, swooping and splashing through the water.

Twyla tried to cheer her up. "I thought that would totally crack you up…like, with laughter, not with actual cracks."

"Oh, hi, sorry, Twyla," said Rochelle, finally realizing her friend was beside her. "I was just dreaming about what it's like to…"

"Spend hours coming up with unappreciated rock jokes?" Twyla suggested.

"No." Rochelle laughed. "What it's like to do *that*." She pointed at Lagoona gliding through the water in a game of tag with Sirena.

"I guess gargoyles can't swim, huh?"

"No, I'd sink right to the bottom. But I bet it's amazing."

Twyla looked across the pool at the Plankton Prep

team. "Well, those guys can swim and they don't seem all that happy." One of the defeated swimmers flopped to the floor, his eight legs sprawling around him.

Spectra Vondergeist materialized at the edge of the pool, a pencil and a notebook in her ghostly hand. She was frantic. "Okay, story, I need a story. Just one story…"

She saw her friend Clawdeen the werewolf by the Fear Squad and flew over to her. "Okay, ghouls, who's got a story? I've got the need for leads. Gimme the gossip, gossip, gossip! Gotta scoop?"

"Whoa!" Clawdeen was taken aback. "Slow down, Spectra. What's the matter?"

"I'm trying to come up with something new to post to the *Ghostly Gossip*—and I've got nothing! It's been nearly two weeks since my last blog update and my readers are getting very impatient."

Ghoulia groaned from the bleachers.

"I'm working on it!" answered Spectra, flustered. "Ah!" She threw up her hands.

Clawdeen shook her head. "Don't worry, ghoulfriend. I've got your back. After this meet is over, I'll help you find a good story. I promise."

"That is so sweet, Clawdeen." Spectra sighed. "How come you're always there for me?"

"S'what ghoulfriends do." Clawdeen smiled.

But Spectra didn't relax. She was anxiously

scanning the crowds in the stands. "I'm gonna
go check with the ghosts. Maybe they've heard
something." She flew off, up into the bleachers toward
Johnny Spirit, Operetta, and Scarah.

Spectra hovered above them. "Come on, ghosts.
You've got to have a story for the *Ghostly Gossip*. The
word *ghost* is right in the name. Operetta?"

The fashionable phantom thought about it. "Let's
see…*ooh*! 'Kay. Manny Taur and Iris broke up, then
got back together. And they—"

Spectra shook her head, disappointed. "Old news.
I need something fresh."

"I heard Mr. Hack bites his toenails," offered
Johnny.

"Ew!" screamed the ghouls.

"I said *fresh*, not gross," Spectra reprimanded him.
"Besides, Mr. Hack's toenail biting isn't news—it's
common knowledge."

Spectra's eyes darted along the rows of students
sitting in the bleachers. Toralei, the werecat, was
looking particularly unhappy. Maybe she had the
scoop on a hot rumor.

"Hey, Toralei," she said, flying over. "Got any news
for my blog?"

Toralei hissed. "Here's some news…you cheat
on *one* essay in Creative Frighting class and you get
suspended from Fear Squad for an entire month."

Down on the deck, Clawdeen did a backflip and the crowd roared with approval.

Toralei's green eyes narrowed. "Actually, Spectra, I do have some gossip." She leaned close to Spectra and whispered in her ear.

Spectra gasped. "Now *that* is a genuine health concern that my readers need to know! I have my story!"

The ghost vanished through a wall to dash off her blog post.

Toralei plastered an innocent smile on her face and waved sweetly to Clawdeen. Clawdeen waved back, suspicious. She didn't trust that cat, but before she could give it any more thought, Frankie Stein called together the Fear Squad.

"All right, ghouls, a perfect pyramid will knock 'em dead!" she shouted.

A buzz of iCoffins resounded through the stands. Everyone was getting an update at the same time.

"New post on the *Ghostly Gossip*!" exclaimed Twyla, excited.

Rochelle was already reading it. "'*Take care, loyal readers. This reporter just got a hot tip that the werewolves of Monster High have fallen victim to an outbreak of were-fleas...*'"

All around the pool, kids were checking their iCoffins and freaking out.

"Were-fleas?" Deuce jumped up, terrified.

"Dude!" Heath exclaimed to Clawd. "You've got were-fleas?" He scooted away.

"Ew, gross!" shrieked a ghoul.

"Keep 'em away from me!"

Toralei looked particularly upset. "Oh dear, were-fleas? Better steer clear of the werewolves."

The ghouls in the Fear Squad pyramid could hear everything. Cleo couldn't believe it. How could her friend not have told her? "Were-fleas? Clawdeen, you have were-fleas?"

"That's ridiculous!" insisted Clawdeen.

Still, Cleo was trying to edge away from Clawdeen—and the pyramid began to shake.

"Cleo! Stop shaking!" Frankie pleaded.

At the top, Draculaura couldn't maintain her balance. She was swaying back and forth. "Hey, what's going on down there?"

"I do not have were-fleas! That's not even a thing," explained Clawdeen.

But no one was really listening. Everyone was panicking. Frankie tried to tell them to be still, but it was too late. The pyramid collapsed with a giant *splash* right into the pool.

From the stands, Toralei smirked. If she wasn't going to be on the Fear Squad, at least nobody else would be either.

The Fear Squad ghouls emerged, soaking wet, from the water. Frankie's bolts sparked and shocked everyone. "Oops! Sorry!"

Clawdeen shook herself off. Everyone in the whole pool was whispering and staring at her and her siblings. *I think I need to talk to Spectra*, she decided. Without drying herself off, she bounded away in search of the gossip ghoul. So much for the diving team victory—this was a catastrophe!

CHAPTER 2

A SPOOKY SIDEKICK

In the hall, students were slamming shut their lockers and getting ready to go home. Draculaura stared at her soaking wet pom-poms, gave them a quick wring, and tossed them into her locker with her Fear Squad bag. As she turned to go, a floating bouquet of roses blocked her way. "Ahh!" screamed Draculaura, startled.

Johnny Spirit materialized from behind the flowers. "Oh, hey, sorry, Draculaura."

"Johnny Spirit! You scared me half to life!" exclaimed Draculaura. Her pulse was racing.

"Sorry about that," the ghost apologized. "Clawd just asked me to give these to you. He's got were-fleas or something." He pointed down the hallway where Clawd was standing, scratching his arm.

Draculaura looked longingly toward her boyfriend. But he ordered her to stay away. "I'm probably contagious!" he told her.

Draculaura took the flowers from Johnny. "Tell Clawd thank you for the roses. But seriously, don't scare me like that."

Johnny shrugged. He couldn't help it if he was startling sometimes. "Anyway, some of the other ghosts and I are going to go float around at the Maul this afternoon. You and Clawd are welcome to join us." Operetta and Scarah were coming down the hall, chatting together.

"I'll have to catch up with you," explained Draculaura. "I'm almost finished here." She pulled out her pom-poms and gave them another wring as Johnny flew off with his friends.

Draculaura took a towel from her bag and tried to dry off her things. A gust of wind blew down the hall and gave her chills. Someone must have left a door open somewhere. She looked down the hall but everyone had left. It was a little eerie being the only one still in school. She could have sworn she heard someone whispering behind her.

"Hello?" she called. "Is someone there?"

No one answered. The school was quiet and spooky. She shut her locker and turned to walk away when she felt the wind again and heard her locker creak open. She whirled around.

"Johnny Spirit? Is that you?" She looked up and down the empty hallways. No one was there. "I told you not to scare me…"

She took a deep breath and shut her locker again, giving it an extra push shut. But before she'd gone halfway down the hall, the locker burst open and all of her belongings floated out and swirled into a cyclone. Draculaura screamed, racing as fast as she could toward the main entrance. But before she reached the front door, she remembered something, turned around, ran back toward the tornado, reached her hand into the circling mass of her things, grabbed her lip gloss, and ran out of the school to find her friends.

By the next morning, Draculaura had almost completely forgotten about her exploding locker. It had probably been Johnny playing a joke on her. Still, she felt a little nervous as she headed back into school. Especially when the doors opened by themselves when she was coming up the steps. She didn't remember them being automatic—and they weren't when Manny Taur walked up to them.

Even stranger were the gusts of wind that seemed to follow her around throughout the day. She was flipping through a magazine in Mr. Rotter's study howl when the pages began flipping…all by themselves. The magazine opened to a page of a vampire model in a pretty haunt couture dress. Draculaura couldn't believe it as her pen floated into the air and, all by itself, circled the outfit. Huh? What was going on?

Later in the day, just before lunch, the wind became wilder and blew her hair up into a flip and swirl and a completely new freaky style. Her friends couldn't believe it when she arrived in the Creepateria.

Rochelle looked up from her lunch. "Your hair looks claw-some, Draculaura. How'd you get it to do that?"

"I don't know," answered Draculaura, sitting down. "You'll have to ask my ghost friend."

The ghouls looked expectantly at Sirena. Sirena, who could be a bit of a daydreamer, loved Draculaura's hair. "Okay, I don't remember doing that, but apparently I'm an amazing hairstylist."

Draculaura shook her head. "No, you ghouls, I think…I think I'm being haunted!"

Everyone gasped.

"Haunted? Are you sure?" whispered Twyla.

Draculaura's napkin floated into the air, unfolded itself, and gently dropped across her lap. Her fork and knife began cutting up her lunch on their own. "Pretty sure," answered Draculaura.

Rochelle turned to Sirena. "You're half ghost. Do you know anything about hauntings?"

Sirena looked very thoughtful. "Hmm," she said. "My grandmother used to say that you could get rid of them by holding your breath."

Draculaura took a deep breath and held it. She waited. Nothing seemed to happen.

"Or maybe that was hiccups," added Sirena.

Draculaura exhaled, frustrated.

Twyla shook her head. "Maybe we should talk to one of the other ghosts about this."

Something was happening to Draculaura—and none of her friends knew what it was.

CHAPTER 3

DON'T LOOK NOW!

Out on the front steps, Spectra was working on her gossip column. But every time she was about to type up a story on her laptop, she would reconsider. She needed something really juicy this time, but she hadn't written a word.

Clawdeen came over and sat down beside her. "Ghoulfriend," she began, her voice serious. "We've got a problem."

Spectra sighed. "You've got that right. I am going through the worst case of ghostwriter's block in history. I've got nothing to write about!"

Clawdeen exhaled. "I'm talking about the story you posted yesterday. About the were-fleas?"

"Oh yeah, how's that going?" asked Spectra innocently. "You're not still itchy, are you?"

"There's no such thing as were-fleas!" Clawdeen explained. "That's just a gross rumor somebody made up. Bad gossip!"

"Oh." For the first time, Spectra realized that she might have hurt her friend.

"And I know you didn't mean anything by it," said Clawdeen. "But you've got to be more careful posting rumors like that. You gotta check your facts."

Spectra felt terrible. "I am so sorry," she apologized. "You're, like, the best ghoulfriend. I'd never want to cause any problems with my stories."

Deuce, Heath, and Manny bounded up the steps past the ghouls.

"I heard Slo Mo didn't come to school because he had geist-lice," Heath was saying.

Spectra began typing furiously—but Clawdeen stopped her. "You're doing it again."

Spectra shut her laptop. "Sorry."

"Listen," advised Clawdeen. "I meant what I said before. I'll help you find a story."

"Thanks, Clawdeen. I just get frustrated sometimes. Great stories don't run up from out of nowhere, you know."

Draculaura and her ghoulfriends burst through the front doors, all talking at once. Rochelle rushed over to Spectra. "Draculaura's being haunted!"

Sirena gazed across the school grounds. "I'm not sure how I'm supposed to feel about it. I'm only half ghost so…I guess I'm half scared?"

"Haunted?" questioned Spectra. "No, there's no way she's being haunted."

"We all saw it!" explained Twyla. "Draculaura is being haunted by a ghost."

Spectra squirmed. "Are you sure? Maybe it was just the wind?"

Draculaura pointed at her new hairdo. "Could the wind style my hair like *this*? Don't get me wrong, it's super cute—but still!"

Spectra was unnerved. At Monster High, ghosts were welcomed—why would a spirit choose to haunt a fellow student?

"Are you okay, Spectra?" asked Twyla. "You look white as a ghost. You know, like more than usual."

"It's not possible," said Spectra, biting her lip. "It can't be a haunting. That's against the rules."

"Rules? Which rules?" Rochelle asked.

"Is there something you're not telling us?" added Clawdeen.

Spectra was trying to figure something out. "Don't worry, Draculaura. It won't happen again. It…it just won't happen again." She floated back inside the school.

Sirena smiled happily. "All right, then! Problem solved. What's next? Oh! How about we help Clawdeen with her flea thingy?"

Clawdeen was annoyed. "Come on, let's see where she's going." The girls followed her back inside as she muttered to herself. "Were-fleas! Were-fleas!" She couldn't help it. She just had to scratch her arm every time she thought about them. And they weren't even real!

CHAPTER 4

WALK TOWARD THE LIGHT

Spectra checked to make sure no one was following her. She looked over her shoulder one last time as she flew up a ladder that led to Monster High's attic.

Clawdeen and the ghouls rounded the corner just in time to see Spectra's ghostly feet disappearing above them. They quietly climbed the ladder behind her so she wouldn't realize they were there.

The attic was filled with abandoned trunks, forgotten paintings, and furniture covered in dusty sheets. Spectra glided over to a wooden crate, reached inside, and pulled out a hidden key. Clawdeen and the ghouls crouched behind a cobweb-covered wardrobe, spying on her. Twyla disappeared into the shadows.

Spectra levitated up a spiral staircase in the center of the attic. It led to a sheet-covered window high up near the beams. She was inserting the key into an invisible lock when she heard something. What was it? She looked around the room. Nothing. She must be hearing things.

Draculaura held her breath. She had gasped when a red silk scarf, hanging from a coatrack, had mysteriously drifted across the attic and wrapped itself around her throat. But it didn't seem like Spectra had seen them.

The ghouls watched as Spectra turned her key and revealed a smaller, dustier room above the attic. It, too, had a sheet on the ceiling. Spectra pulled it away, exposing a large hole in the roof. Brilliant white light poured through it in a column to the attic floor.

Blinking, the ghouls watched as Spectra hovered next to the beam of light. What was she doing? What was happening? Spectra closed her eyes, took a deep breath, and disappeared into the glowing column. The light grew brighter and brighter—and Spectra was gone.

The ghouls emerged from behind the wardrobe, stunned.

"Oh my ghoul! Where did she go?" whispered Draculaura.

Rochelle shook her head. "Do you think she's okay?"

"It's like she just vanished!" exclaimed Twyla.

Clawdeen approached the beam of light.

"Are you sure that's a good idea?" Twyla warned.

"No," answered Clawdeen. "But I promised Spectra that I'd help her find a story. And whatever she's after, I'm not letting her go alone." She walked into the light and disappeared.

It only took a moment before the other ghouls found their courage and stepped into the beam as well.

The walls of the attic faded away; the light grew brighter and brighter. Where were they?

The light became a glowing river, rising straight up, up, up to the sky. The ghouls, too, were ascending— and they discovered themselves on the deck of a ship, plowing vertically through waves of light. Somehow they didn't fall off the boat, as if all the laws of gravity had changed. Behind them, the walls of Monster High disappeared.

"Where are we?" gasped Rochelle.

The sky darkened. Wind began to blow. Waves rocked the boat. A black raven fluttered through the air and landed on the ship. "Caw!" it shrieked.

The ghouls jumped in fear.

"Hello?" called Draculaura. "Is anybody there?"

Looming in front of them was a dark figure, carrying a long staff and robed in black like the Grim Reaper.

Draculaura gulped. "Um…is anybody *else* there?"

CHAPTER 5

A GHOST STORY

The ghouls cowered. This was the end. It was over. All over.

"Okay, well, this was fun…" whispered Draculaura to her friends.

The sky grew even darker. A deep voice boomed over the roar of the wind. "You are not supposed to be here…"

The ghouls trembled, terrified. They never should have followed Spectra.

"Seriously," said the reaper. She whipped off her black hood—and instead of the Grim Reaper, the ghouls saw a cute, bubbly ghost. The sun immediately began to shine. "I don't think you're supposed to be here."

The ghouls were confused.

"Sorry about that!" apologized the ghost. "I get carried away with this whole 'reaper' thing sometimes. I'm River! River Styxx!"

Rochelle was the first to recover. "Nice to meet you, River."

"U-um…" stuttered Twyla, searching for something to say. "Nice boat?"

"Thanks!" gushed River, perfectly friendly now. "It's my dad's. Usually he's the one who ferries ghosts between the two worlds, but he's at a reaper convention in Las Plagueas. So until he gets back, this baby's my very own party ship to the Ghost World!"

She extended her staff to hit a hidden button and music began to play. River twirled the staff like a baton in time to the pulsing beat, the raven bopping up and down beside her.

Clawdeen looked up in the sky where the boat was headed. "I'm sorry, did you say *Ghost World*?"

"You ghouls aren't supposed to be here!" It was Spectra!

"Yes," said Twyla drily. "The dancing reaper made that quite clear."

River giggled. "Did somebody say confetti cannons?" She hit another button with her staff and four cannons emerged from the hull of the ship and let loose sprays of rainbow-colored confetti.

"Spectra, what's going on?" Clawdeen was baffled.

Spectra bit her lip, concerned. "You have to promise not to tell anyone." She held out her hand and the other girls placed theirs over hers in a solemn pledge. "There's another world—a Ghost World—where all the different types of ghosts come from. There are phantoms like Operetta, banshees like Scarah...even faceless ghosts like my old friend Kiyomi Haunterly."

"And don't forget us reapers!" bubbled River Styxx.

Draculaura was confused. "How come we've never heard about this Ghost World?"

"It's a secret," explained River, "because most ghosts are pretty nervous about outsiders. You're what ghosts refer to as...Solids."

Twyla tapped Rochelle's rock-hard arm. "Solids? Eh, her story checks out."

"Most ghosts have never even seen outsiders from the Monster World," Spectra added. "They'd probably be pretty scared if they saw you. Except for Sirena, of course."

The mermaid ghost was peering over the edge of the boat at the cannons. She pressed a button, and there was another explosion of confetti. She was surprised to find everyone staring at her. "Sorry, got distracted. I'm totally listening."

Spectra gave her a questioning look. "My family left Ghost World a long time ago," she told her friends. "They thought Monster High would be a good place for me. But this boat will take us back to my old school—Haunted High."

She pointed up across the bow of the ship. Another school was appearing in front of them— made of iridescent bricks with shimmery towers and translucent archways.

"Unbelievable!" Clawdeen's mouth dropped open. "A whole school sitting right above Monster High!"

"So?" asked River, turning to Spectra. "What brings you back to Ghost World?"

Spectra paused for a moment, taking a breath. "Draculaura is being haunted," she said at last.

"That's impossible!" exclaimed River. "Ghosts don't haunt the Monster World. There hasn't been a haunting since…" Her voice dropped to a hushed whisper. "…since the Red Lady."

Goose bumps prickled on the arms of the ghouls.

"The Red Lady?" asked Rochelle.

River pulled her dark hood over her head. Her voice dropped dramatically. "The legend of the Red Lady is a story that every ghost learns when he or she is young."

The ghouls shivered. Clouds covered the sun. The waves turned choppy. The weather responded to River's moods.

"Hundreds of years ago, the Red Lady was the scariest, most notorious ghost in the Monster World,"

River told the ghouls. "Boo York, Scaris, Fangcouver…
no one was safe from her hauntings."

River swirled her staff in the river. An image arose
in the waters of a woman in a hooded red cape, her
face hidden.

"They say," continued River, leaning close to the
ghouls, "that the Red Lady figured out a way to
quickly travel between the Ghost World and the
Monster World."

In the river, the ghouls saw a vision of the Red Lady
appearing before two Frankenstein monsters—and
terrifying them. Scenes of her frightening vampires,
werewolves, and ghouls of all kinds swirled through
the waters.

"The Red Lady became more infamous with
every ghostly crime. Nothing delighted her more
than hiding in the shadows, waiting for just the
right moment to"—River vanished into thin air and
materialized an instant later right behind the ghouls,
scaring them out of their wits—"scare unsuspecting
outsiders," finished River. "But one day, her scaring
spree finally came to an end when the Red Lady was
captured and locked away. They say that the weight of
her crimes was so heavy that it will take her centuries
to pay her debt to society."

The ghouls were hanging on River's every word.
When she had finished, there was silence—until River

pulled off her hood and smiled. Instantly, the sun was shining again and the waters were smooth.

River twirled her staff playfully. "Sorry, I just love a good ghost story."

Draculaura shivered. "Yeah, me too."

"Anyway," continued River, "that's why there aren't hauntings anymore. No ghost ever wants to face the same fate as the Red Lady."

BOOM! Out of nowhere, a cannon exploded!

"What was that?" screamed Twyla.

"You ghouls better hold on to something," warned River.

BOOM! Another explosion burst through the air.

The ghouls gasped as a massive floating pirate ship blotted out the sun and cast a terrifying shadow over River's ship. It launched another cannonball! *BOOM!* The ship lurched, hit by the blast.

"Ahhh!" screamed the ghouls.

The pirate ship ploughed toward them, pounding the side of the ship with a huge wall of water. The boat rocked from side to side and the ghouls struggled to maintain their balance. A glamorous ghost with a sword, a pirate hat, and a peg leg peered at them. On her shoulder was a one-eyed cuttlefish. At her side were four glowing skeleton pirates.

"Yar har har! Prepare to be boarded, ya unseaworthy brine shrimp!" cackled the ghost pirate girl. The skeletons at her side rattled their bones and chattered their teeth. She grabbed a glowing rope that hung from the mast of her ship and swung down to the ship.

She pulled out a stopwatch and clicked it. "Yar har har!!! Thirty-seven seconds. A new record!"

"New record! New record!" parroted the cuttlefish.

She whipped out a transparent piece of paper and thrust it toward River. "Would you be so kind as to sign this for my ghost pirate class?"

River dashed off her signature and handed it back.

The pirate girl waved it over her head triumphantly. "I am Vandala Doubloons, captain of the *Salty Specter*, fiercest ghost pirate on the haunted seas. And I'm very seasick!" She lunged toward the railing of the ship to steady herself. She closed her eyes, clearly woozy. "C'mon, Vandala," she said to herself. "Get it together. Nobody likes a seasick pirate…"

Vandala took a deep breath, exhaled slowly, and opened her eyes. She blinked. She shut her eyes and opened them again. She dived below deck, screaming, "Solids! Solids! Solids! You have Solids on your boat!"

"It's okay, Vandala," said River reassuringly. "They're, um, nice Solids."

Vandala cautiously poked out of the cabin. "You're sure they're not here to haunt me? I've been handling a lot of cursed treasure lately."

Draculaura was amazed. "Spectra, if this is how ghosts at Haunted High are gonna react to us, maybe we should just wait for you on the ship."

Spectra shook her head. "No, it should be fine as long as you're with me. But it wouldn't be a bad idea to disguise you ghouls so you don't attract too much attention."

River smiled. She knew just the disguise!

CHAPTER 6

POLTER-GUESTS

The *Salty Specter* and the Grim Reaper's ship glided up to the docks next to the school. A group of ghouls emerged on deck in hooded black robes that hid their faces. Like a flock of crows, they glided across the gangplank and headed toward the front door of Haunted High.

Draculaura tugged at her robes. "You're sure you don't have something a little less grim? Perhaps in pink?"

River shook her head. Her remote chirped as she locked up the ship.

In front of them was a massive, ornate door to the gothic building—except that it didn't have any doorknobs. The ghosts—Vandala, River, Sirena, and Spectra—passed through it effortlessly. The rest of the ghouls stood there staring at it. How were they supposed to get inside?

"A little help?" Twyla sighed. She knocked on the door.

Instantly, Spectra flew back out. "Whoops! Sorry!"

Spectra tapped the door and the heavy stone became transparent. The ghouls walked through into the main hall of the high school.

Sirena loved the school. "Oh my ghoul, it's boo-tiful!"

The walls were painted in glimmering pastel colors that shone like opals. The main hall soared up, up, up with hallways and classrooms branching out from heavenly levels. Ghost students flittered and hovered, leaving lingering trails of shimmers behind them.

"I can't believe my parents never told me about this place." Sirena sighed. "I wonder if there's a mermaid world I don't know about."

Clawdeen was impressed. "Too bad you have to keep this a secret, Spectra. This would be something worth blogging about."

"You're right," she agreed. "But there's no reason I couldn't start a second blog just for the Ghost World. I could call it the *Haunted Herald*!" She took out a pad and began scribbling down notes.

Draculaura was trying to befriend Vandala. She

complimented her pet. "I like your…um…fish guy."

"He's a cuttlefish," said Vandala. "His name is Aye."

"Aye?" repeated Twyla.

"Aye aye!" said Vandala with a wink.

"Aye!" repeated the cuttlefish.

Spectra was happy to be back in her old school. "It's exactly as I remember it. Nothing's changed since I left."

"Well, almost nothing," noted River. She pointed across the hall with her staff. A pair of ghosts was dragging heavy, glowing chains behind them.

"That's a strange fashion statement," commented Rochelle.

"Those are detention chains," explained River. "Courtesy of Principal Revenant."

"Detention? They're being punished?" Spectra was aghast.

River nodded. "If you get caught breaking the rules, you get chains that you have to work off. Sometimes with extra homework, sometimes with chores."

"I had to swab the floors for months," chimed in Vandala, "to work off my last detention."

A ghost student whizzed past with a barrel of potatoes chained around his neck. He was peeling them as he flew; he looked miserable. A lot of the ghost students seemed unhappy.

"There are lots of different types of chains," said River. "But they all work the same way. As long as you're in detention, you can't leave Haunted High."

"All right, ghouls, somebody here has to know something about Draculaura's haunting," said Spectra. "I say we hit the Creepateria and ask around."

Vandala's cuttlefish saluted. "Aye aye!"

The girls hurried off—but they didn't see a shadowy figure watching them from the very top of the hall. The arrival of the ghouls had been noticed.

CHAPTER 7

A BOO'S WHO GUIDE TO HAUNTED HIGH

The Creepateria was as impressive as the main hall—tall and windowed with plenty of room for ghosts to float about. Tables were stacked and went up, up, up right to the ceiling.

"This place is incredible!" enthused Sirena. "Are you sure *this* is the Creepateria?"

A ghost student wafted past with a tray of food.

Clawdeen sniffed. "It's the Creepateria."

An elegant ghost in a flowing kimono-inspired outfit flew into the room. Everyone seemed to know her.

"Hi, Kiyomi!"

"Kiyomi! Over here!"

"Another great outfit, Kiyomi!"

Her skin was a brilliant blue—but her face? It wasn't there. Where it should have been was just a smooth, shimmery expanse.

"Wow, who's the popular ghoul?" asked Twyla, impressed.

"Wait!" exclaimed Spectra. "*That's* Kiyomi? I'd recognize that face anywhere...well, you know what I mean." She called out to her long-lost friend.

The moment Kiyomi spotted Spectra, her face turned a vibrant red. She swooped over and wrapped her friend in a welcoming hug. "Spectra! You're back!"

"And you're...different! You used to be the shyest ghost at Haunted High. Now look at you, all fashionable and popular."

"Hey, change is good, right?" Kiyomi twirled like a model and a pampered pet, Kaiju, poked out of her purse.

Spectra introduced her ghoulfriends. Kiyomi became suddenly shy when she met Draculaura, but she quickly recovered.

Draculaura felt odd around Kiyomi. "You seem familiar to me. Have we met before?"

Kiyomi's rosy blush turned to a nervous green. "I don't think so."

"Are you okay, Kiyomi?" asked Spectra. "You're turning green."

"Yes, I'm fine," she said. "I'm sorry, I've got to fly, but let's catch up before you leave. Nice to meet you all." Kiyomi zipped away across the Creepateria and vanished down a hallway.

"Your friend is so colorful," Draculaura commented.

"That's how Kiyomi shows her emotions, how she expresses herself without a face," explained Spectra.

"Well, she didn't stick around very long," noted Clawdeen.

"Yeah," agreed Vandala. "You know us popular types. Always rushing away, late for something…" Her voice trailed off as she noticed the way everyone was staring at her. "What? I'm popular. I've got more than six hundred mateys on Insta-groan." She held up her iCoffin to show her profile pic—a selfie taken next to an overflowing treasure chest.

Spectra wanted to get back to business. "It's fine. We're not here for classmate reunions. We're here to help Draculaura."

Spectra made her way over to a lunch table and her friends followed, careful to keep their hoods over their faces so no one would know they were Solids. As they sat down, Spectra turned to the other ghosts. "So…

anyone hear about somebody haunting the Monster World?"

Her question was like a bomb. Everyone at the table stopped eating and stared at her.

"What do I look like?" said one student finally. "The Red Lady? That's against the rules."

"Oh, I know. Just heard a rumor, that's all," said Spectra, recovering.

Clawdeen raised an eyebrow. "And if there's one thing Spectra knows about, it's rumors."

Spectra looked at Clawdeen guiltily.

A boy ghost at the table was curious about what Spectra had said. "Who would even want to go to the Monster World? Those spooky Solid kids give me the creeps." He shuddered.

Draculaura, Clawdeen, Rochelle, and Twyla sank deeper into their hoods.

A commotion across the room turned everyone's attention away from the ghouls. Dozens of spray-paint cans were hovering by themselves near a wall, releasing mists of luminescent paint.

"What's going on?" Spectra wondered.

"Oh, it's just Porter," said River Styxx.

The paint cans were spiraling while a bucket of paint was swinging back and forth, splashing the wall with dashes of color. Slowly, a picture emerged of ghost hands breaking a chain in half. The artist himself also materialized as he worked—and he was a particularly good-looking poltergeist, even if he did have detention chains wrapped around his waist. He stepped back to admire his creation and splashed another dab of paint onto the wall.

"He is kinda cute," said Sirena dreamily.

"Cute or not, is he allowed to paint on the walls like that?" Spectra wondered.

"He is not," snapped River Styxx, "and here come the hall moanitors."

The three hall moanitors—Past, Present, and Future—swooped into the Creepateria. They wore shiny black badges on their chests. A heavy, ancient book floated next to Past. Future was concentrating, with a finger pressed to his temple.

Rochelle gulped. They were scary. "The hall moanitors? What do they even do?"

River surprised the ghouls by jumping up behind them and making them scream. "That's what they do. The ghosts of hauntings Past, Present, and Future are Principal Revenant's eyes and ears around the school."

River pointed at the moanitor with the book. "That's Past. She keeps track of every student infraction at Haunted High. Present, the leader, is always on the lookout for someone breaking the rules. And the ghost of the Future, he has a way of predicting what you're gonna do before you do it."

Vandala shivered. "Just the sight of those scalawags shivers me timbers."

Present peered at Porter's graffiti art. Past stopped behind Present—and Future bumped into her. Present glared at them both before tapping on his badge to communicate with the principal. "Principal Revenant. We've got a fourteen twenty-four in the Creepateria."

A voice blared through the badge. "It's the paintergeist again, isn't it?"

Porter saw the moanitors floating toward him and grinned devilishly. "Ah, come on! It's ghost paint. It's not permanent." He waved his hand through the paint—which rippled like water and vanished.

But that didn't stop the moanitors.

Porter whistled. "You're gonna have to catch me first!" He swooped through the Creepateria.

"I hate it when they run," moaned Past.

Porter weaved around the floating lunch tables, a triumphant smile on his face. He was having a great time.

Spectra was captivated. "A bad-boy artist on the run from the law. I might have just found my first story for the *Haunted Herald*." She whipped out her pad and began scribbling notes.

Porter dove straight toward the ground where she was, but she didn't see him coming.

She was talking to herself and writing. "Maybe I can get him to give me a quote..."

But before Spectra could finish her thought, Porter crashed into her and they both tumbled to the floor. Paint cans tipped and splattered. Somehow Spectra kept writing.

The moanitors were out of breath after the Creepateria chase, but now a giant disembodied ghost head was looming over the students. The woman's face was stern and her gray hair was pulled back in a tightly wound bun. "Hello, students," she said in a grim voice.

The kids looked down at their hands. They were scared of her.

"*Hello*, students," said the head again.

"Hello, Principal Revenant," responded the students obediently.

A dark smile turned up the corners of Principal Revenant's thin lips. "Porter Geiss. Treating us to another one of your little art projects?"

Past, the hall moanitor, flipped through her book. "That's the fourth time this month, Ms. Revenant."

"I knew she was going to say that!" exclaimed Future.

Principal Revenant's eyes narrowed. "He'll never learn his lesson if he doesn't pay the price. Isn't that right, students?"

"Yes, Principal Revenant," intoned the students.

Present tapped his badge. A detention chain lined with scrub brushes flew through the air and attached itself to Porter. He sank under the added weight of the new coils.

"Thanks a lot," he said to Spectra, as if it were her fault that he'd been caught.

"Hey! You crashed into *me*!"

Principal Revenant noticed Spectra. "You, I don't recognize. Are you one of my students?"

"No, ma'am," said Spectra innocently. "I'm Spectra Vondergeist. I'm just visiting from Monster High."

There were gasps throughout the Creepateria.

River Styxx winced. "Maybe shoulda left that part out."

But Principal Revenant was very interested in this news, *too* interested. "Really? So there are ghost students who go to school in the Monster World? How interesting. And your little reaper friends there? They attend Monster High as well?"

The ghouls nodded, keeping their heads down and hoping the hoods obscured their faces.

Principal Revenant squinted. "Awfully shy, aren't they?"

All at once, the ghouls' hoods flew off their heads. The entire room went wild with panic.

"Outsiders!"

"Solids!"

"What are they doing here?"

"Well, I guess that werecat's outta the bag," muttered Clawdeen.

There were cries of alarm.

"What do they want? They're here to haunt us!"

An expression of wicked delight lit up Principal Revenant's face. "Moanitors? What is the punishment for bringing non-ghosts to Haunted High?"

"Whoa!" said Spectra. "Punishment?"

Past was flipping through her book. "Um… technically there has been no rule that says you can't bring in non-ghosts. It's never happened before."

Principal Revenant turned to Present. "Make a rule," she ordered.

Present grabbed Past's book and began scrawling across the page.

"But that's not fair!" shouted Spectra. "You just made that rule up!"

"She does that," Porter whispered to her.

"Not helping!" hissed Spectra.

Future was about to make a prophecy. "Look out for the paint—"

Before he could finish, Porter levitated the cans into

the air and hurled them at the moanitors, covering them in paint. He framed them with his fingers, like he was a movie director. "Another brilliant work of art." He laughed. "Think I'll call it…" He turned to Spectra. "*You ghouls should get out of here while you can.*"

It was a brilliant diversion!

The ghouls didn't hesitate. They dashed out of the Creepateria as fast as they could. It was time to escape Haunted High.

THE HOT NEW
STYLE AT HAUNTED HIGH—
GHOST COUTURE!

SPIRIT RALLY!

PARANORMAL ACTIVITY AT THE BOOGIE MANSION!

NO ESCAPE!

KIYOMI TO THE RESCUE!

VANDALA DOUBLOONS, CAPTAIN OF THE *SALTY SPECTER*, AND AYE, HER TRUSTY CUTTLE•SH

RIVER STYXX—DAUGHTER OF THE GRIM REAPER!

Can Porter outwit Principal Revenant and the hall moanitors?

GHOST BUSTED

MONSTER HIGH

River's ready to rattle some chains.

CHAPTER 8

WHAT GHOST UP MUST COME DOWN

Principal Revenant watched calmly as the ghouls fled. She almost seemed amused.

Out in the hallway, Kiyomi saw them speed past, and her no-face turned an even deeper shade of green.

Spectra tapped the door to make it transparent and the ghouls ran out, relieved to be out of Haunted High.

"Good trip," said Twyla sarcastically. "We'll have to do this again sometime."

They raced toward River's boat. As soon as they were onboard, River hit the throttle, and the boat roared away from the dock.

Draculaura looked over her shoulder and saw the moanitors flying toward them. "Hey, ghouls. We've got a trio of grumpy ghosts headed this way, fast."

"Maybe they just want to party?" River pushed a button and confetti exploded out of the cannons.

"Ha!" shouted Vandala. "Now we're talkin'!"

The moanitors were already covered in ghost paint, and the confetti stuck to them when it hit. It stuck to their heads, their hands, their tongues.

"Ptha!" spat Future, trying to get confetti out of his mouth.

Furious, Past and Present tapped their badges and detention chains spewed toward the boat.

But the chains flew right through Rochelle and Clawdeen. As if they were ghosts.

"I guess they only work if you *are* a ghost!" said Rochelle.

"Good thing," joked Clawdeen. "I don't think I have a single pair of shoes that goes with detention chains."

The boat sped down, down, down through the river of light.

River Styxx brought the ship to a stop just above the hole in the attic. "Okay, it's been a pleasure!"

The beam of light brightened and flashed.

The ghouls tumbled through it, landing with a *thud* on the floor of the attic.

"We made it!" Rochelle was relieved.

"Never thought I'd be so happy to see this creepy old attic." Clawdeen sighed.

But Spectra didn't look happy—at all. "I'm sorry we didn't figure out who was haunting you, Draculaura. But don't worry, we'll—"

Before she could finish what she was saying, detention chains flew out of the light, lassoed Spectra, and pulled her back into the light.

"Spectra!" screamed the ghouls. They grabbed for her, but the chains were more powerful.

"Hang on, Spectra!" shouted Clawdeen.

"Don't let go," begged Rochelle.

"Spectra!" shrieked Draculaura.

"*Help me!*" Spectra screamed.

But it was too late. The ghouls lost their grip and fell backward. Spectra disappeared. She was gone.

"Oh no, no!" moaned Draculaura. "They've trapped Spectra in Ghost World!"

"We have to do something," cried Clawdeen.

"Yeah," whispered Sirena. "But what?"

Clawdeen dusted herself off. "I'll tell you what we're going to do. We're marching right back in there to get back our ghoulfriend."

Rochelle stopped her. "Wait. You heard the new rule—no non-ghosts allowed."

Twyla agreed. "She's right. If we go back, we might get Spectra in even more trouble."

Sirena had a dreamy expression on her face. "So to go back to Ghost World, all you ghouls have to do is turn into ghosts. Ready and...go!"

The ghouls stared at her in disbelief.

"I see a lot of staring but not a lot of turning into ghosts," said Sirena.

"Ghoul, get serious." Clawdeen shook her head. "We can't turn into ghosts."

But Twyla surprised them all by agreeing with Sirena. "No...actually, Sirena's right."

"Thank you!" Sirena beamed. "What am I right about?"

"If we're ghosts," suggested Twyla, "then we're not breaking the rules if we go back. And I know how to do it!"

The ghouls gathered around. Maybe it was possible. Maybe it wasn't. But right now it seemed like the only chance they had of rescuing Spectra.

CHAPTER 9

GHOST-BUSTED

Back at Haunted High, the moanitors had carried Spectra, wrapped in detention chains, to Principal Revenant's office. The office was a long, narrow room at the end of which was a fortune-teller's table. One wall was lined with windows, looking out at the ghost students flitting this way and that through the hallways. The hall moanitors sat at their desks. They were still covered in paint and confetti.

Principal Revenant's head floated behind her table while black robes spread out beneath her. There was a shiny key on the table, like an ebony crystal ball. Spectra sat in front of the table. Three thick books were attached to her chains.

"Well, Ms. Spectra Vondergeist," said Principal Revenant softly. "You certainly caused quite a scene."

Future spat out another piece of confetti.

Principal Revenant glared at Spectra. "Care to explain your little non-specter spectacle?"

Spectra took a deep breath. Surely she could explain all of this. "Principal Revenant, I'm sorry I broke your rule, bringing my friends to Ghost World. But look, I don't belong here anyway. My school is Monster High."

Principal Revenant smiled. "Yes, let's talk about this Monster High. You are not the only ghost who goes there?"

"Well, no," said Spectra, surprised the principal didn't know this. "There are lots of ghosts at Monster High. Every kind of monster is welcome there."

"Hmmm," murmured Principal Revenant. "How very…progressive. Well, I think we are done here. It's going to take you quite a bit of time to work off that detention chain."

Spectra couldn't believe her ears. "How do I do that?"

"By completing ten thousand essays on the complete works of Ghostoyevsky. And then doing it one more time."

Spectra lifted one of the chains, feeling how heavy it was. Even heavier were the books attached to them. "That could take forever! When will I blog?"

Principal Revenant's face was expressionless. "I'm sure I don't know."

Spectra floated toward the door. But she had one last thing to say. If she was stuck at Haunted High, at least she could do a little sleuthing. "Ms. Revenant, you haven't heard anything about any of your students haunting the Monster World, have you?"

Future spat out another piece of confetti. Past and Future stared at her. Principal Revenant's head seemed to grow larger.

"Of course not!" pronounced Principal Revenant. "There hasn't been a haunting since…since…"

"The Red Lady?" offered Spectra.

Principal Revenant's eye twitched. "Yes, that's the one. Terrible, just terrible."

Spectra sighed, picked up her chains, and headed out to the hallway.

Principal Revenant waited until she was out the door before turning to the moanitors. "I had no idea there were so many ghost students in the Monster World. I have a job for you that will enhance our school's attendance…"

From the hallway came the sound of clanking chains.

CHAPTER 10

FRIGHTFULLY FLIRTY

Spectra sat on a bench near the tombstone-shaped lockers. Actually, she wasn't really sitting, she was floating an inch or so above the bench, but she was working hard. She scribbled on her notepad, read what she wrote, ripped the paper, and crumpled it up. She tossed it toward a trashcan, but a hand reached out and grabbed it before it fell in. It was Porter.

He smoothed out the piece of notebook paper and read, "The *Haunted Herald* by Spectra Vondergeist. What's this, homework or something?"

"No," answered Spectra. "Just a blog idea I'm working on."

Porter looked confused. "So you're, like, writing for…fun?"

Spectra smiled. "Sure. I love writing. It helps me…"

Porter shut his eyes and made pretend snoring noises.

"It helps me figure things out," finished Spectra, annoyed. "Makes me feel good. Work out my frustrations."

Porter laughed. "You want to work out your frustrations? You should try painting." He tossed her a spray can.

She handed it back politely. "No thanks. Never been much of a paint-on-the-walls kind of ghoul."

Porter shrugged. "Suit yourself." He took the can and began creating a silly cartoon of a cross-eyed Principal Revenant.

Spectra looked up and down the hallway anxiously. "Isn't that what got you detention chains last time?"

"Relax." Porter laughed. "It's my locker." He opened it. Every surface was covered with his amazing graffiti art. On the locker's floor was a ghost raccoon who peered up at Spectra with dark eyes. He was painting a small corner of the locker, using his striped tail as a brush.

"You always keep raccoons in your locker?" Spectra was intrigued.

"Oh, that's Hue," Porter explained. "He comes and goes. Pretty okay little painter." He shut the locker door carefully. "Artistic temperament, though."

Spectra was interested in this boy. On the spot, she decided to give him her pad and pen. "You should give writing a try. Might keep you out of trouble."

Porter scribbled on the paper. "Hey…you know, this is actually kind of…" He pretended to fall asleep again. "Zzzzzz!"

Spectra shook her head. He was irrepressible—but so cute. "Good-bye, Porter," she said, taking back her pad and pen.

She floated away, but she glanced back to get one more look at Porter. He was hard at work again, putting some last touches to his graffiti. A curl of hair fell over his forehead.

Spectra was so captivated by Porter that she nearly flew into a ghost student slamming shut his locker.

CHAPTER 11

READY FOR THEIR DE-BOO!

Twyla led the ghouls to her home, the boogie mansion. It was very large with lots of wings and annexes. There were doors everywhere. Inside were more doors of all shapes and sizes lining the dark hallways. It was a creepy house—as if the Boogie Man might pop out at any moment, which he might.

"Not much farther," said Twyla. "My dad's study is right up ahead."

Clawdeen couldn't figure out where she was. "It doesn't matter how often you have us over, Twyla, I get lost every time."

"Wait," said Rochelle. "Where's Draculaura?"

"She was just here," said Sirena.

The ghouls stopped in the hallway, listening.

A moment later, there was a knock from a tiny, doll-size door in the wall. Draculaura's face poked through. "I think I took a wrong turn," she said.

Twyla opened a door on the floor and the ghouls tumbled into the Boogie Man's study.

The room was covered in fun-house mirrors that made the ghouls look taller, or smaller, or simply stranger.

Sirena loved them. "This house is fun!"

Twyla pointed at a wardrobe across the room. "In there," she said.

A long distorting mirror covered the wardrobe door, and the ghouls laughed at their misshapen images—except for Draculaura. "Yikes! For once I think I'm okay with not having a reflection."

Yet it almost seemed as though Draculaura *had* seen something in the mirror—a mysterious, ghostly orb. She turned around to see if there was anyone or anything behind her, but nothing was there. She shivered. "Oh good. Still being haunted."

Inside the wardrobe were little glass boxes, each filled with a different kind of sand. There was the kind of sand you find in your eyes when you wake up, sand from the beach, and hundreds of other magical varieties.

"Oh my ghoul, what is this?" asked Clawdeen.

"It's boogie sand," explained Twyla. "My dad uses it

in his work. Each one can change you into a different monster. We just need to find the one that says 'ghost' on it. Can anyone else read boogie?"

Sirena floated up to the top of the wardrobe and removed one of the boxes. "What is this?" she asked. It slipped and fell on Rochelle's head, covering her in sand. *Poof!* Rochelle transformed from a gargoyle into a slimy swamp creature.

"No!" squealed Rochelle. "That's not the right box!"

Twyla pulled over a standing ladder to explore the higher shelves. Clawdeen settled down to wait and pulled out her sketchpad, where she designed new fashions. Rochelle looked over her shoulder, trying to see through her new swamp-monster tentacles.

"*Qu'est que c'est?*" asked Rochelle in French, and then translated. "What's that?"

"I'm trying to write down for Spectra everything that happens. This is gonna make a great story for her blog."

Twyla had found it! Carefully, she climbed down the ladder, a small glass box in her hand. "Rare and ethereal—ghost sand. You ghouls ready to get ghosty?"

"*Oui!*" answered Rochelle, who'd been a swamp monster long enough. "So very ready!"

"So how does this work, Twyla?" asked Clawdeen. "Will it be permanent?"

Twyla nodded. "Yes, until you use a different type of sand. After we save Spectra, we can come back and use the other sands to change back to normal. Draculaura will use vampire sand, Clawdeen werewolf sand…you get the idea."

"Okay, then," said Draculaura. "Let's do this. For Spectra!"

Twyla opened the lid. "Count of three. One…"

Clawdeen sneezed: "ACHOO!" and sand covered everyone! When the dust settled, the ghouls had turned into ghosts. Not only were they transparent, but their clothes had become shimmery ghost fashions.

Draculaura clapped her hands. "Twyla, you're a genius!"

"Draculaura, you're a ghost!" Twyla laughed.

Rochelle spun around, and her weightless dress wafted around her. "Check out our new looks! Totally haunt couture."

Sirena was thrilled that everyone was as see-through as she was. "All right, ghost ghouls, follow me back to Haunted High!"

Sirena spun around in the air, but the other ghouls had no idea how to fly yet.

Draculaura kept lifting up and falling down. Clawdeen pulled her to her feet and sent her careening like a pinball across the room, bumping into furniture and tumbling over herself.

Twyla was spinning round and round in place. "Can't...stop...spinning!" she said breathlessly.

"This is amazing!" enthused Rochelle, diving and tumbling in the air. "I'm weightless! This must be what swimming is like." She rose up, up, up toward the ceiling—and went right through. "Hey, how do I stop?" she called before disappearing.

Sirena giggled. "Oh boy!" Being a ghost was harder than it looked.

While the girls were learning how to fly, the three hall moanitors were standing on the docks by Haunted High, getting ready to unleash an attack on the Monster World. They looked down the light-filled river flowing toward the Solids' school. They nodded at one another. They tapped their black badges. In an instant, snakes of long detention chains slithered through the air, twisting and turning on their way to Monster High.

CHAPTER 12

RUMOR HAS IT...

Spectra peered out of a window at the shining river between the worlds. She was homesick. She tried to open the window, but the moment her hand touched the latch, a purple force field ignited and zapped her. "Ow!"

"Yeah, I've tried that too." Porter had appeared beside her. "But as long as you have that chain, you can't leave the school." To demonstrate, he touched his own hand to the window. *Zap!*

"Yow!" He laughed. "Gotta stop doing that."

Spectra was beginning to realize how serious her predicament was. "So I'm trapped here for eternity? With you." She sighed and floated off down the hallway.

Porter followed her. "Okay, um, I read the *Ghostly Gossip*. You are really good."

Spectra stopped, surprised. "You can read my blog for Monster High here in the Ghost World?"

"Interdimensional Internet," explained Porter.

"'Kay." Spectra nodded. "So now all of a sudden you think writing is a good thing."

Porter stuck his hands in his pockets sheepishly. "Look, I'm sorry I said it was boring."

"I believe your exact words were zzzzzzzzzzzzzzz."

Porter looked embarrassed. "Something like that... Um...so you're some kind of reporter or journalist, right?"

"I like to think so," said Spectra.

"Well, good!" Porter smiled at her. "Because I need help...um...journaling."

This was a strange turn. "I'm not following."

"Principal Revenant," explained Porter. "I know she's up to something. Something bad. I want your help. To find out what it is."

Spectra didn't trust this bad-boy graffiti ghost. "Are you sure it's not just because you don't like her? Back at Monster High there's this ghoul named Toralei and she's—"

"No, it's something else," Porter interrupted. "All the rules and chains she gives out—there's got to be more to it than just handing out detention. It's worse than it's ever been. It's not fair; it's not right. I gotta find out why, but I need help. I need…I need someone smart like you to help me."

Spectra blushed. She was flattered. "So you really liked my blog, huh?"

"Yeah!" Porter grinned. "It was really informative. But what are were-fleas?"

Spectra laughed out loud. Rumors sure did travel fast!

CHAPTER 13

GHOST-NAPPED!

The attic at Monster High was empty, and no one saw the sudden flash that announced the opening of the portal. Light poured through the hole in the roof—and a thick cord of detention chains slithered into the attic, effortlessly slipping through the floor to the school below.

Johnny Spirit, Operetta, and Scarah were chatting between classes. They were worried about their fellow ghost Spectra—she hadn't posted anything on her blog. What was up? Where was she?

"This is gettin' weird," drawled Operetta. "And *not* in the good way."

Scarah agreed. "She hasn't been posting. *So* not like her at all."

A chain unfurled from the ceiling and wrapped

itself around Operetta's leg. She screamed—but it was no use. It was pulling her away.

"Operetta!" screamed her friends.

A second chain snagged Operetta's other leg.

"Help me, Johnny! Don't let me go!" cried Operetta.

"Baby, baby, baby!" sang Johnny.

Chains were slithering like tentacles. Johnny was trapped. Scarah was bound. All three ghosts found themselves yanked through the ceiling into the attic. They were pulled into the light.

"Ahhhh!" they screamed.

Johnny tried to grab on to an old chest, but he couldn't hold on.

Something was reeling them in.

CHAPTER 14

PARANORMAL ACTIVITY

Porter and Spectra were in the library doing research. The shelves hovered in the air. The books glowed.

"This library has records on every ghost who's ever existed in the Ghost World. If Ms. Revenant is up to something, we might find some kind of clue by looking into her past." Spectra flew over to a ghost computer and started typing.

Porter watched her admiringly. "How do you know so much?"

"I've done my time in libraries," answered Spectra without looking up.

"Hey, I spend time in libraries too," said Porter.

Spectra shook her head dismissively. "Reading? Or painting graffiti?" In fact, that was exactly what he was doing—spraying a design on one of the bookshelves.

Porter waved his hand over the paint. It vanished.

Meanwhile, Monster High's team of ghouls-turned-into-ghosts was arriving at the docks of Haunted High.

River secured the ship. "I just can't get over your new ghost looks," she gushed. "Floaty, freaky, cute!"

"Thanks!" responded Rochelle. "I think we're starting to get the hang of it." She began drifting over the side of the boat into the river, and Sirena pulled her back onboard.

As they floated up the dock toward the main entrance of Haunted High, the ghouls struggled to control their new ephemeral forms—but it was easier to get through the front door.

Inside the school, class had just let out, and ghost students were heading to their lockers.

"Uh-oh," gasped Clawdeen as a flood of ghosts poured around her, sending her spinning like a top. Rochelle began drifting up and couldn't stop. Twyla whizzed across the hall at top speed.

"I can't stop!" cried Clawdeen.

"Little help over here," Twyla begged.

Rochelle reached out her arms, trying to find something to hold on to. "I knew we should have practiced more!"

Luckily, Kiyomi and Vandala spotted them. "Hey,"

called Kiyomi. "Spectra's ghoulfriends are back!"

Draculaura managed to get herself halfway stuck inside the floor so only the top part of her was visible.

"They look like they need a little help," Kiyomi whispered to Vandala.

Vandala couldn't believe it. "A fish flopping on the deck needs a *little help*. Those ghouls need all the ghost help they can get."

Lost in research in the library, Spectra had no idea her friends were so close. She had surrounded herself with open books and records.

Porter had stacked up a few books as well—and he was tapping on them like a drum set and singing. "*Porter and Spectra, crackin' the case! Solvin' lots of mysteries all over tha place!*"

Spectra glared at Porter.

"What? I'm working on our theme song," he defended himself. "All good duos need a theme song."

"So we're a *duo* now?" Spectra said drily.

"Yeah! I paint and write the theme songs—and you do all the boring reading and writing stuff." He executed another drumroll with his hands.

Spectra ignored him and flipped through a book. "Nothing." She sighed.

"Nothing bad about Principal Revenant?" asked Porter.

Spectra's brow was furrowed. "Nothing at *all* about

Principal Revenant. There's no record of her at all. Like she never existed."

"Weird," said Porter.

For once, Spectra agreed with him. "It doesn't make sense. There are records here about everybody. About you, about me—tons of stuff about the Red Lady…"

Porter looked serious. "If there's no record of Ms. Revenant, then that could only mean one thing…"

Spectra waited expectantly.

Porter leaned close to her and whispered, "I think she's a…ghost!" He burst out laughing.

Spectra flew out of the library. She was not amused!

"C'mon, it was a little funny," said Porter, flying after her. "Seriously, though, if there's nothing there, that totally proves she's up to something."

Spectra turned to him. "I don't know. Maybe there's nothing to find. Maybe she really is just a regular principal trying to make a positive difference at her school…"

They drifted around a corner to see Principal Revenant welcoming a new group of ghosts to Haunted High—Johnny Spirit, Operetta, and Scarah. In the Ghost World, they were paler and more transparent. They were also wrapped in detention chains.

"Welcome, new students! Welcome!" said Principal Revenant, a cold smile on her enormous face.

"I know those ghosts!" Spectra whispered to Porter. "They all go to Monster High. What are they doing here? Why are they wearing detention chains?"

"I think you'll feel right at home at our school," Principal Revenant was telling the new arrivals. "We're always on the lookout to take in bright new ghost students like you. Welcome to Haunted High!"

Porter pulled Spectra aside. "See? There is no way that she is not totally and completely up to something."

Spectra frowned. Porter was right. Something was wrong about all of this. Very wrong.

"Haunted High is lucky to have you." Principal Revenant's voice was sickeningly sweet. "Now, off you go, then. You don't want to be late for ecto-nomics!"

The principal's giant head dissolved.

Spectra immediately flew over to her friends.

Operetta hugged her. "Spectra! So they got you too? 'Splains the blog."

"I don't understand." Scarah was close to tears. "One minute—Monster High. Then all of a sudden we're hit with these chains and pulled to the Ghost World."

Johnny was totally confused. "Some kind of mandatory transfer, I guess."

"I don't want to be here. I want to go home," wept Operetta.

"Don't any of you ghosts worry," said Porter, joining them. "Spectra and I are on the case."

The ghouls wiped away their tears to get a good look at this handsome new ghost.

"Oh, this is Porter," introduced Spectra.

Porter wrapped an arm around Spectra. "We're a duo."

Spectra slipped through his arm. "We are *not* a duo." She tried to comfort her friends. "Just sit tight, and we'll figure out what's going on."

As Spectra flew off in search of evidence, Porter turned back to the newcomers. "Duo," he whispered with a wink.

Operetta and Scarah exchanged a glance. What was going on between Spectra and this poltergeist?

CHAPTER 15

CREEPY CRACKDOWN

Kiyomi steered the out-of-control ghosts to the Haunted High swimming pool. It was just like Monster High's pool—except the water floated on the ceiling and swimmers dove upward.

Kiyomi was trying to teach the ghouls how to fly. "Okay, let's do it again. Just like before. First we go up…" She rose gracefully into the air.

Clumsily, the ghouls tried to imitate her. They weaved and wobbled, but with a little concentration, they managed to control themselves.

"And then we go down…" said Kiyomi.

The ghouls hovered above the floor.

"Very good, just like swimming!" instructed Kiyomi. "Now we go left."

Unfortunately, Draculaura floated *right*, bumped

into Clawdeen, almost passed through her, and ended up getting stuck to her.

"Left, Draculaura, left," said Clawdeen, irritated.

"I know, I know, I'm trying," said Draculaura, struggling to separate herself. Eventually, she managed to follow Kiyomi around the pool. "You are so spooky sweet to help us out, Kiyomi. You didn't have to do all of this."

Kiyomi's face turned a rosy blush. "Yeah, Draculaura. I kind of did."

"All right, ghouls, I think we're ready. Let's find Spectra," said Clawdeen.

Sirena wasn't so sure. "I didn't realize how tricky flying would be for someone who's never done it before."

Rochelle gazed up at the pool above their heads. "Now that I'm weightless, there's something I just have to try." She tucked herself into a ball and hurled herself upward. "Cannonball!"

A yellow shimmer rippled where she splashed, bathing everyone in its shiny glitter.

Rochelle flew back to join the others who were applauding for her.

"Aw, I love that," said River Styxx.

"I'm more of a swan-dive fan myself," admitted Vandala.

The others couldn't believe it.

"What?" said Vandala, surprised. "I've gotta like everything that's pirate?"

The ghouls were finally ready to fly to the Creepateria—and look for Spectra.

It was lunchtime, and she was already there with Porter. Always keen to eavesdrop on gossip, Spectra couldn't believe what she was hearing.

The ghosts were talking about the new students who had just arrived.

"I heard those new ghosts were kicked out of Monster High because ghosts aren't welcomed there," said one student.

"Somebody told me," said another, "that they came here to warn us that those creepy Solids want to come up here and take over Haunted High."

"Yeah," agreed someone else. "I heard they want to suck us up in vacuum cleaners and put us in cages and feed us crackers."

Spectra stopped at their table. "Gossip is garbage," she scolded them. "You have no idea what you're talking about. None of that is true. Those are just dumb rumors. Dumb. Hurtful. Rumors."

She heard herself and couldn't help but remember the rumors she had spread in the past. Gossip could be dangerous.

"Something wrong?" asked Porter.

"No." Spectra sighed as she sat down at a table.

"Just thinking about something a friend told me."
She looked up to see that very friend flying into the
Creepateria. "Oh my ghouls! My ghouls! You came
back!"

Clawdeen flew to her—and passed on through.

"You're ghosts!" Spectra couldn't believe it.

"Yeah, long ghost story," said Clawdeen, joining her
at the table. "But don't worry. I took notes." She held
up her sketchbook.

Twyla glanced around the room, on the lookout for
the hall moanitors. "But right now we've got to get you
out of that chain and back to Monster World."

Spectra bit her lip. "Things just got a lot more
complicated. It's not just me. All of the ghosts from
Monster High are stuck here too."

"What?" gasped Clawdeen.

Draculaura couldn't believe it. "Here at Haunted
High?"

"What do you mean?" asked Rochelle.

Porter jumped in. "It's Principal Revenant and
those hall moanitors. They're up to something."

The moanitors were patrolling the Creepateria.
Present pulled a student from his seat.

"You there," he barked. "It's against the rules to…
um… Let's see… You were…"

Past interrupted. "Flying in a Red Zone."

"Flying in a Red Zone," said Present officially. "Good one."

"He's not gonna like that," warned Future.

The student exploded just as Future had predicted. "*Red Zone?* What does that even *mean?*"

"Told you," said Future.

Present tapped his badge, and chains wrapped around the student before he could complain again. He collapsed back into his chair.

Kiyomi was appalled. "This is getting out of hand. They're giving detention for everything now. Look at how many chains there are in here."

Students were covered in them. The troublemakers were in chains, as were the kids who never got in trouble. They clanked and jangled. The school was beginning to look like some kind of old-fashioned prison.

Present glided over to Kiyomi and pulled her from her seat. "Don't you know staring is against the rules?"

Kiyomi was baffled. How could she possibly stare at anyone? "Staring? No, I don't even have a face. I wasn't…"

Present pursed his lips. "Hmmm. Okay, then. Talking back to a hall moanitor is your offense."

"That is also against the rules," noted Future.

"Detention it is," announced Present.

Draculaura was not going to stand for this injustice. "You can't give her detention. She didn't do anything."

"Another troublemaker," stated Present. "Past, please pull up this student's permanent record."

Past thumbed though her ghost tome but couldn't find anything. She double-checked the index, she flipped through the pages, she studied Draculaura suspiciously. "Wait a minute…"

Past tapped her badge and spoke into it. "Principal Revenant, we have a situation here."

The principal's giant head materialized in the Creepateria.

"These ghouls!" shouted Past. "They're not ghosts. At least they weren't before. These are the Solids!"

Ms. Revenant's eyes widened. She looked as if she might gobble up the ghouls in front of her. "You've turned yourselves into ghosts," she said with surprise. "I need to know how."

Almost imperceptibly, Porter shook his head. He was trying to warn the ghouls.

The ghouls gulped, frightened. What should they do?

Principal Revenant's head became bigger and more threatening. "You will tell me how to turn monsters into ghosts," she ordered.

The moanitors tapped their fingers to their badges. "Don't!" screamed Porter.

"Stay outta this, paintergeist," ordered Present.

"Do it," Principal Revenant said gleefully.

Chains flew toward Draculaura. She shut her eyes and braced herself. But Kiyomi leaped in front of her and took the hit instead.

"Draculaura! Fly!" Kiyomi cried.

The ghouls didn't need to wait a second longer. They sped out of the Creepateria, the moanitors racing after them.

Principal Revenant watched the chase, but she was distracted. Discovering that monsters could become ghosts changed everything. Everything. Her beady eyes sparkled with evil plans.

CHAPTER 16

HIDE AND SHRIEK

The ghouls were racing toward the main entrance as fast as they could, weaving in and out of surprised students. Porter led the way. The very moment the moanitors rounded the corner, he made a hard right, vanished through a wall, and the ghouls followed.

They found themselves in another hallway that went straight up. They barely had time to catch their breath before the moanitors materialized through the wall, chains already extending from their badges.

"Incoming!" warned Vandala.

The ghouls rolled and flipped to avoid the chains, thankful for Kiyomi's flying lessons.

"Go right!" ordered Porter, vanishing through another wall.

The ghouls merged through the wall, and Porter took them straight down through the floor. The moanitors split up, each heading in a different direction.

"We're just flying in circles," cried Spectra. "Do you actually have a plan?"

"Trust me," urged Porter.

Future burst through a set of lockers right in front of them, and the ghouls skidded to a stop. "Heh, heh, heh," chuckled Future. "I saw this coming!" He put his finger to his badge—but before he could release more chains, the locker beside him, glimmering with yellow haze, slammed open, bonking him in the face.

Future was stunned. "I did not see that coming!"

Porter and the ghouls whizzed past him and took refuge in the library. Porter pointed at a wall of bookshelves. "There! In there!"

Porter dove into the bookshelf. The ghouls were right behind him. By the time the moanitors had caught up with them, there was no one in the library. Where had they vanished to?

The ghouls found themselves in a secret room without any doors. Every wall was covered in Porter's graffiti art and there were paintings on easels. The beautiful, intricate art shimmered and glowed.

"Un-boo-lievable!" whispered Sirena.

Twyla gazed around the room. "This must have taken ages to paint."

Porter shrugged modestly. "I had a little help."

Spectra was impressed. "Porter, I knew you were an artist, but I didn't realize…Wow."

Porter was pleased, but there were more pressing problems. "You ghouls will be safe in here," he told them. "Nobody knows about this room but me."

Rochelle noticed a bunch of furniture covered in drop cloths. "What's all this back here?"

"Just some furniture that was here when I found this place. Never had any use for it," he explained.

Rochelle whipped off a dusty sheet and revealed an intricately carved desk, more bookshelves, and some rough wooden crates covered in cobwebs. Everything looked like it had been abandoned centuries ago.

"Oh, such a beautiful antique desk," Spectra said.

Clawdeen was trying to figure out what had just happened. "So why do you think Principal Revenant went all crazy about turning monsters into ghosts?"

"Yeah," agreed Kiyomi. "What does she want with that boogie sand?"

There was a moment of stunned silence. This was news. They hadn't told anyone about how they had transformed themselves. No one else had even been there.

"We didn't tell you about the boogie sand," said Twyla, confused.

But Draculaura realized something. "No way!" she exclaimed. She studied Kiyomi, shaking her head. It all made sense at last. "You were there! You were the orb I saw in the mirror at the boogie mansion. *You* are the one who has been haunting me!"

Kiyomi blushed a deep forest green. "Um…I… Yes…s-so sorry," she stuttered.

No wonder Draculaura had felt like she'd met Kiyomi before when she first came to Haunted High. "But why?" she wondered.

"I wasn't trying to haunt you or scare you," explained Kiyomi, embarrassed. "I just love what I see at Monster High. The fashion, you are all so cool with your freaky flaws, so nice to each other. And talk about fangtastic style."

"We are pretty stylish," Draculaura admitted.

"I used to be so shy," continued Kiyomi. "But spending time with you ghouls at Monster High…I don't know, made me feel more…colorful."

Draculaura understood—she went over to Kiyomi and gave her a warm, ghostly hug. Being haunted was no big deal, really.

Kiyomi glowed a warm, contented blue. "I wanted

to tell you. But then Spectra got detention chains and I felt so guilty because I was the reason you all came here."

"It's not your fault, Kiyomi," Draculaura reassured her. "It's that no-good principal."

"Yeah," agreed Clawdeen. "What are we gonna do? We can't hide in here forever."

Spectra nodded. "No, we can't. This has to stop. I'm going to talk to her."

She was headed toward the wall when Porter stopped her. "You can't!"

"Someone has to make Principal Revenant realize she's going too far," said Spectra, determined.

"But she's…scary! She may do anything!"

Spectra lifted up her chains and let them drop with a *clang*. "I already have detention chains. What's the worst that could happen?"

Porter touched her arm. "I could lose you," he said softly.

The other ghouls turned away, trying to pretend they weren't in the room.

"Whoa," whispered Twyla in a soft voice. "Bad boy's got a soft spot."

But Porter's romantic plea was not going to make Spectra forget her friends. She had gotten them into this mess—and she was going to get them out of it.

"I'll be fine, Porter," she said. "I have to do this. For them." She vanished through the wall.

Since arriving in the room, Sirena had been enraptured by the graffiti, barely listening to what her friends were saying. But now it suddenly hit her. "Wait a minute," she gasped. "We didn't tell Kiyomi about the boogie sand! That must mean…Kiyomi is the one haunting Draculaura!"

CHAPTER 17

A DEAL WITH THE DEVIL

Spectra flew to Principal Revenant's office. She was about to open the door when she overheard voices.

The principal was yelling at the moanitors. "You lost them! Argh! To be able to turn all monsters into ghosts! Exactly what I need! I could double our attendance!"

Present dared to voice a concern. "But won't the students become suspicious with that many new ghosts arriving at Haunted High?"

"Leave the students to me." Principal Revenant chortled. "I'll manage the rumor mill…"

Spectra's courage vanished at the chilling sound of Principal Revenant's voice. She pulled out her notebook to record what she'd heard.

But Future was right behind her. "Get all that?"

Spectra screamed and leaped through the door—right into Principal Revenant's office.

In front of her was a ghost with a normal-size head. It was the *real* Principal Revenant—not her projected image—and her entire body was covered in detention chains. Chains wrapped around her arms and her legs. Chains were slung over her shoulders and wrapped around her waist like belts. She had chains on her head and chains on her feet. Spectra couldn't believe it. What did this mean?

Principal Revenant was staring at Spectra greedily. "Well, well, what do we have here?"

Future snatched Spectra's notebook out of her hands. "Somebody fancies herself a junior reporter."

But Spectra barely noticed her lost notebook. "You're wearing chains," she said, dumbfounded.

"I'm wearing *a lot* of chains," answered Principal Revenant coldly. She hovered toward Spectra, pulling a seemingly endless trail of chains behind her. They rattled and scraped along the floor. She got up close to Spectra's face. "Do you like them?" she hissed. "I'm more than happy to share them with you, dear."

Obediently, Present went to press his badge—but a ghost raccoon burst through the wall. He skittered along the walls, streaking paint. Paint cans flew into the office and began spraying by themselves. The moanitors stumbled about, grabbing at the cans.

"Porter!" Spectra exclaimed with delight.

He materialized in the room. "Get out of here!" he yelled.

Spectra slipped through the door amid the confusion.

"Enough!" screeched Principal Revenant.

The key on her desk flew through the air into her hands. She held it in her palm as it glowed. The chains on her own body released—and wrapped themselves around Porter, imprisoning him.

Porter's paint cans crashed to the floor. Principal Revenant hovered over him. "Now, Mr. Geiss, tell me where your little Monster High friends are hiding."

"Yeah, good luck with that," he spat insolently. He twisted and turned, but he could not break free.

"If you tell me, I might be able to get rid of some of those chains," she said with mock sweetness.

She was tossing the key up and down. An enormous, heavy chain coiled over Porter and weighed him down. He strained against it—and she sent another. And another. And another. He could barely move at all.

"All right," he gasped at last. "Maybe we could make a deal."

Principal Revenant smiled in triumph. She always won.

CHAPTER 18

BOO-TRAYAL

The ghouls waited in Porter's hidden art studio—with no idea what was happening. Kiyomi's Kaiju was entertaining them by pretending to be a Godzilla monster stomping through a city made out of spray-paint cans. Every time he roared, the ghouls giggled. He was adorable.

Draculaura was getting to know Kiyomi. After all, they'd been spending a lot of time together. "So you were able to watch us at Monster High without traveling across the river?" she asked.

"The Ghost World and the Monster World are more closely connected than anyone knows," she explained. "By...I don't know, some kind of energy. And some ghosts can use that energy to open little windows between the worlds."

Kiyomi took a deep breath and concentrated. In front of her, a circular window in the air opened. It shimmered with yellow energy—and through it the ghouls could see a hallway in Monster High. There in front of them was their friend Hoodude, not even aware that he was being watched, scratching his behind.

Embarrassed, the ghouls looked away.

"It's usually more interesting than this," Kiyomi apologized. She closed the portal.

Draculaura realized something. "Windows between worlds. That must be how the Red Lady was able to haunt the Monster World."

"Very likely," agreed Kiyomi. "I shouldn't do it. Every time I open a window, I risk revealing the Ghost World to the Monster World."

"I still don't understand why that's a bad thing," said Draculaura.

"There are a lot of ghosts who are scared," Kiyomi explained. "They really believe that the Solids are all out to get them. It would start a riot! And until somebody can convince those ghosts that they're wrong, I have to keep this power a secret."

Draculaura grinned at her new friend. "Maybe they just haven't met the right Solids yet."

Kiyomi glowed blue with happiness. She couldn't

believe how accepting and sweet Draculaura was being to her. But before she could ask if everyone at Monster High was like Draculaura, Spectra rushed back into the room.

"Principal Revenant!" she said breathlessly. "Planning something! And then I got caught, and she has all these detention chains…and then Porter—"

"Told me exactly where to find all of you," announced the chilling voice of Principal Revenant, her giant floating head looming over the ghouls.

The moanitors had also found them, and detention chains were flying around the room, imprisoning the ghouls. Chains immobilized everyone—even Vandala's little cuttlefish.

But it was not the chains that were making Spectra's eyes well up with tears—it was the betrayal. "He told you?"

"I offered to reduce his detention for good behavior." Principal Revenant laughed. "So he gave you up very easily…"

Spectra struggled against the chains. "No," she insisted. "That can't be true. I don't believe you."

Principal Revenant regarded her contemptuously. With an evil snicker, she summoned Porter. His chains were gone—all gone. Principal Revenant was right.

"How could you?" asked Spectra, heartbroken.

"Oh, you know how those bad-boy types are. They only care about themselves," said Principal Revenant cruelly.

The hall moanitors chuckled.

Ghostly tears cascaded down Spectra's cheeks.

"Spectra…" whispered Porter. "I—"

"Don't!" ordered Spectra. She floated right through Porter, as if he wasn't even there, and vanished from the room.

"Oh, Spectra!" gasped Clawdeen, sad for her friend.

It was bad enough to be trapped at Haunted High forever—but even worse to be stuck there with a broken heart.

CHAPTER 19

A MONSTROUS MISSION

Haunted High was on lockdown. Panicked students listened as Principal Revenant's giant head made the announcement.

"By now you must have heard gossip that intruders have viciously attempted to invade our beloved school. Well, I'm here to tell you that these rumors are… absolutely true!"

Ghosts clutched each other in fear. This was too terrifying for words—their worst nightmare was happening. Solids were invading them.

"They've come to frighten us," warned Principal Revenant, reveling in their terror. "To haunt us! To destroy our ghostly way of life!"

From the pool to the Creepateria, from the lockers

to the classrooms, students listened in stunned silence to the news.

"But rest assured," oozed Principal Revenant, "your principal is working on a plan that will end their treacherous plot to destroy us!"

Cheers erupted around the school. Principal Revenant disappeared.

But then her face flashed back into view. "Oh," she added. "I'm being told that tomorrow is haunt dog day in the Creepateria!"

More cheers echoed through the halls of Haunted High.

Back in her office, the real Principal Revenant flicked a button on her wrist that turned off the device projecting her head to the school. It was time to deal with more interesting matters—punishing ghosts.

Principal Revenant floated over to the window, her chains dragging behind her. The hall moanitors were back at their desks. Present was filling out all of the necessary detention paperwork while Past lounged, her feet up on the desk, playing a video game. Future was building a house of cards with a Tarot deck.

Principal Revenant was biding her time, but still there were things she needed to know. "Now then," she said without looking at the ghouls. "It's very important that you ghouls tell me how you've turned yourselves into ghosts."

"Why should we tell you anything?" protested Twyla.

Principal Revenant whirled around, ready to make a deal. "Because if you tell me, I'll reduce your sentence. Those detention chains could be much lighter."

"You'll have to do better than that," scoffed Clawdeen. "You can't buy us off like that no-good, backstabbing, traitorous paintergeist." She glanced at Spectra. "Sorry, ghoul."

Spectra shrugged listlessly. "It doesn't matter."

Principal Revenant glowered. "One way or another, you *will* tell me," she threatened.

The bells and whistles of Past's game began ringing, and Principal Revenant fumed. "Seriously?"

Past looked up, realizing she was in trouble. "Sorry," she said meekly. "The ghosts in the game got me. Ironically…"

But before she could finish, Principal Revenant had snatched the game from her hands and crushed it in her grasp.

The coils of chains draped over her body shuddered and rattled. Another length of chain emerged, like a new tail. It was as if the chains were growing.

Alarmed and furious, Principal Revenant saw Clawdeen's sketchpad. "What's that? What are you doing there?"

Clawdeen looked up from where she'd been scribbling. "Taking notes," said Clawdeen defiantly. "When all this is over, my ghoul Spectra is gonna write a story telling the world what kind of principal you really are."

"Confiscated!" snapped Principal Revenant. The pad flew out of Clawdeen's hands into hers—and she flipped through the notes. "*Wicked? Evil?* My dear, you flatter me." She continued reading, however, becoming more and more curious. "Interesting. The boogie mansion…"

With a gasp of horror, the ghouls realized what she'd discovered.

"Boogie sand!" she exclaimed. "Thank you, how very enlightening." She tossed the notebook at the moanitors, hitting Past in the face. "Head to the Monster World at once," she ordered them. "And get to the boogie mansion as fast as you can."

The room darkened as if a storm were about to break. River was furious. "And just how do you expect them to get there? Because I'm certain Past, Present, and Future are stuck right here without me to ferry them across…"

Even as she spoke the words, River realized her mistake. It was a matter of a moment before she heard the moanitors gunning the engine on the ship. Party music blared across the water. They were motoring away on her boat. "Well, that's annoying," she griped.

BOOM! The sound shook the walls of Haunted High. The moanitors were firing the confetti cannons.

"Okay, that's just rubbing it in." Twyla sighed.

The ghouls collapsed under the weight of their chains, defeated.

Students passing in the hallway were gossiping about the lockdown. "What do you think Principal Revenant's plan is?" asked one.

"I don't know," said the other. "But I'm glad someone's keeping us safe from those Solids."

Somehow, hearing this made everything worse. No one even knew what was really going on. Principal Revenant had fooled them with rumors.

"I'm sorry my notes gave away the boogie sand," said Clawdeen. "I was just trying to help Spectra."

Kiyomi shook her head. "No, this is *my* fault. I never should have opened those windows to Monster High."

"Don't blame yourself, Kiyomi," said Draculaura. "If I hadn't been such a scaredy-bat, Spectra wouldn't have come back to Haunted High in the first place."

Spectra hovered away from the others. She didn't like what she was hearing one bit. No one had done anything wrong—except for one person. "This is somebody else's fault." She sighed angrily. She stormed out of the office, determined to find Porter.

The ghouls gathered up their chains as she marched through the air to Porter's locker. She disappeared through the door; passed through the ghost paint, dissolving the graffiti; and stormed into the library. She was on a mission. Next stop: Porter's secret studio.

Porter was putting the drop cloth over the furniture when Spectra burst into the room. Porter looked delighted to see her. "Spectra! Good, you're back. We have to talk."

Spectra's hands were on her hips. "You've got that right," she replied.

Porter noticed her fury—and her ghoulfriends at her back. "I know you're all really angry with me," he hurried to explain.

"Angry doesn't even begin to describe what we're feeling, paintergeist," Draculaura exploded.

"I understand!" Porter said, holding up his hands. "But if you'll just—"

"Oh, you understand," sneered Rochelle. "Must be pretty hard to understand when you've got paint for brains."

Twyla slapped her palm. "Nice!"

"Spectra," begged Porter. "Please."

The pain on Spectra's face was evident. "You know,"

she said, her voice steely. "It's one thing to hurt me. But what you did affected all of my ghoulfriends. And that's a line that you just don't cross, Porter."

Porter protested. "But…I…"

No one was interested in listening to his excuses. Sirena removed Vandala's cuttlefish from her shoulder and let it loose. "We've had enough!" she announced. "Go get him, little fish guy!"

The cuttlefish swam over and slapped Porter's feet with its fins. The ghouls were screaming at him all at once.

"Can I just show you something?" yelled Porter.

The ghouls were quiet. The cuttlefish gave him one last squelchy slap.

"This better be good." Spectra sighed.

Porter grinned. He paused. In his hands was Principal Revenant's shiny key. He must have stolen it—but how?

Porter touched it and every link on every chain began to glow. The chains began to unwind and release the ghouls—before flying over to Porter and tightening themselves around him.

The ghouls were in shock. They couldn't believe it.

Rochelle had no problem with it. "Okay, that's pretty good."

"I had to make a deal with Ms. Revenant," Porter

explained. "So I could see how this key thing works. Then, I kinda, you know, borrowed it…so I could get you all out of detention."

Spectra was looking at Porter in a whole new light. "I don't know what to say…"

He grinned. "I figured out from watching Ms. Revenant that the detention chains can't be broken— only transferred to another ghost using this key. It is set to transfer them to me. I think it's made of the same stuff as the hall moanitor badges." Porter handed the key to Spectra. "Here. You can use it to free the Monster High ghosts and take them back to Monster World."

Spectra beamed. "You're just full of surprises, aren't you?"

"Yeah, I guess," Porter said modestly. "Here is one more surprise." He turned to a drop cloth hanging near the wall.

When he tugged on the drop cloth, he revealed that the old desk and bookshelves had been transformed. Porter had painted them in bright, cheerful colors and set up a computer. There was a nameplate on the desk. It said SPECTRA.

Porter looked pleased and a little bashful. "I thought you might be able to use this. You know, for writing."

Spectra gazed in wonder, first at the desk and then

at Porter. Her mouth was open but she couldn't find any words.

"Do you like—" began Porter.

Spectra interrupted him with a hug. She clanked against his heavy chains, but it didn't matter. Porter was the best.

Porter coughed, embarrassed. He took a breath, trying to keep his cool. "All right, then." He coughed again. "Very good." He tried to lean nonchalantly against the wall but slipped right through it with an enormous crash. Somebody was love-struck!

CHAPTER 20

WRAITH TO THE RESCUE

A ghost anchor descended from the Grim Reaper's ship and sank into the lawn outside the boogie mansion. The moanitors didn't lose any time tearing through the house in search of the magical sand. They found the collection in the wardrobe without too much trouble. The only problem was that none of them read boogie. How were they going to figure out which box would turn the monsters into ghosts?

Past grabbed a random box and opened it. She flicked a few grains of sand onto Present. *Poof!* Instantly, Present was transformed into a squealing pig monster with a curlicue tail. Present grabbed another box with his pink hoof and dumped the entire contents on Past's head. *Poof!* Past was a snarling, fur-covered yeti!

"I knew it was gonna do that," announced Future smugly.

Past and Present grabbed boxes of sand and hurled them at Future. *Poof! Poof!* He turned into a zombie, and before he could stagger one step, he transformed into a tiny tiki monster. *Poof!* He hurled a box of sand at Present—who became a jack-in-the-box.

Sand was everywhere! The moanitors were turning into every kind of monster in the world—except ghosts.

Back at Haunted High, Principal Revenant was supervising a ghost game among the students. She was distracted as she waited to hear from the moanitors.

One of the students was trying to solve a missing-letter word puzzle. The ghost gave a long, wailing moan and everyone watching applauded. The "boo" was correct.

Present barged into the classroom, out of breath. "Principal Revenant," he gasped. "We have the ghost sand."

"Excellent!" she gloated. "Now I just have one more job for you…" Her voice trailed off as a vampire duck waddled into the room.

It was Future. "I don't want to talk about it!" he yelled.

Out in the hallway, Spectra was going over the plan with the ghouls one last time. "Step one—we round up all of the Monster High ghosts and get rid of their chains. And quickly before Ms. Revenant realizes we have the key."

"Right," agreed Twyla. "Step two, we take Vandala's ship to the Monster World and get my dad's boogie sand back from those moanitors."

"And step three," completed Vandala. "We sail the *Salty Specter* to the Scaribbean in search of the legendary sunken treasure of Davey Bones!"

The ghouls stared at her. What was she talking about?

"I'm thinking maybe we should stick to one adventure at a time," suggested Clawdeen.

Vandala sighed, disappointed. "Yeah, you're probably right. Sorry, Aye," she whispered to her cuttlefish.

"Aye," he answered sadly.

"All right, ghouls," rallied Spectra. "Let's rattle some chains." She tossed the key up into the air and caught it like a practiced pitcher. The ghouls vanished into the wall to begin their mission.

They didn't have to wait long until Johnny Spirit staggered out of class. He was struggling under a load of heavy chains and books that banged into him as he walked. As he passed by a portrait of an old ghost elder, a hand reached out through the painting and grabbed him. He stared up at the stern painted face in terror—and saw Draculaura's pretty smile shining through. He collapsed with relief and she dragged him by his chains through the wall.

In a nearby classroom, Operetta was unhappily working on a huge stack of papers connected to her chains. She couldn't believe it when Rochelle peeked through the door, quietly summoning her. Without a word, she lifted her papers and followed her friend. Where were they going? Were they trying to escape?

Spectra was waiting for them by the main door. The key was in her hands, and the moment she saw Johnny and Operetta approaching, she activated it. Their chains flew off! They high-fived each other in celebration. Without a word, Spectra motioned them to fly out the door.

They were followed by an exultant pair of Monster High ghosts who, only moments before, had thought they would be stuck forever cleaning the floors with toothbrushes—until Clawdeen rescued them. Spectra made their buckets and their chains vanish.

Scarah was the last ghost left to find, and she was high up at the very top of the building washing windows. Every now and then Principal Revenant's head would float by and order her to work harder.

But Twyla found her. She waited until Principal Revenant was gone, and then emerged from the shadows—startling Scarah. Twyla held her fingers to her lips and beckoned her friend with her finger. Scarah didn't hesitate. She dropped her squeegee brush and flew after her.

More and more ghosts from Monster High were floating out the main door, released from their chains by Spectra. They had to shield their eyes from the sun as they emerged outside, but Sirena carefully guided them down to the docks.

Vandala welcomed everyone onto her boat. "The *Salty Specter* is ready to set sail for Monster High!"

The freed ghosts cheered. "Hip hip hooray! Hip hip hooray!"

"I can't believe it." Draculaura sighed with relief. "We're finally going home."

Twyla paused, noticing something. "Wait, where's River?"

"Right here!" She laughed, jumping up behind them and startling them.

All the ghosts were onboard, but Spectra still wasn't ready to leave. "Vandala, can you wait for just a minute? I need to see Porter."

"Awww!" gushed her ghoulfriends.

"Calm down," she said seriously. "I just need to say thank you one more time."

"Awwww!"

"Stop that!" she said a little more firmly. "I'll be right back."

She zipped away as the skeleton pirates watched her go. "Awwww." They sighed.

Spectra snuck back into Haunted High and found Porter in a corner of the main hall. He couldn't move. He had taken on everyone's detention chains.

The sight of him broke Spectra's heart. "Oh, Porter! I just wanted to say thank you. For everything. Without you, all of my friends would be stuck here."

Porter tried to be cheerful. "Hey, it was both of us. Working together. We make a pretty good duo."

"Yeah, we do," said Spectra shyly.

Porter tried to lift his hand to her, but the weight of the chains was too much for him. They looked into each other's eyes.

"I promise I'll come back," vowed Spectra. "You know, to break in that fabulous desk."

"And maybe one of these days I could come see you at Monster High?" Porter asked.

"I'd like that," Spectra whispered. She laughed. "But you should probably leave your paint cans here."

It was hard to leave him. She knew she had to—everyone was down in the boat waiting for her. But just as she turned to go, Principal Revenant's voice boomed over the loudspeaker. "Attention, students of Haunted High. Please report to the auditorium for a mandatory Spirit Rally."

That is strange, thought Spectra. "Spirit Rally? What do you think that's about?"

"Get out of here while you still can," urged Porter.

But Spectra changed her mind. She was loyal to her Monster High friends—but the ghosts of Haunted High also needed her help.

"No!" begged Porter as Spectra flew toward the auditorium. He wanted to fly after her, but his chains were holding him back. "Man, these are heavy!"

CHAPTER 21

CHAIN OF EVENTS

Porter staggered after Spectra to Haunted High's auditorium. The stage floated in the middle of the room and there were no seats—just students with their legs crossed floating in rows. Almost all of them were covered in detention chains.

Spectra couldn't believe it. "Look at all those chains."

"The hall moanitors have been busy," said Porter, coming up behind her.

Kaboom! Something exploded, filling the room with dark smoke. When it had cleared, Principal Revenant's projected head was staring at everyone from the stage. "Hello, students!"

"Hello, Principal Revenant." The students' voices were obedient but weary.

"For centuries we have lived in fear of outsiders," Principal Revenant lectured. "And now they have come to our school to haunt us! To frighten us!"

"Boo!" moaned the students together.

"I know, I know!" Principal Revenant was acting like she was on their side. "I have a plan to keep all of you safe from the outsiders—once and forever!"

The crowd cheered, directing all of their unhappiness at the outsiders. Spectra glanced at Porter, concerned. What was Principal Revenant up to?

"As we speak, our noble hall moanitors are traveling to Monster High. They are carrying a special powder that I created that will permanently transform all of those students into ghosts!"

Spectra shuddered. "So that's why she wanted the boogie sand?"

Principal Revenant's dark eyes glittered. "When they are ghosts, I'll give them well-deserved detention chains—as punishment for sinister Solid scheming!"

Everyone applauded. This was what they wanted! Principal Revenant had convinced them that everything was the fault of Monster High!

"As your principal always says," she continued, becoming increasingly maniacal, "they'll never learn their lesson if they don't pay the price. Isn't that right, students?"

"Yes, Principal Revenant," the students answered. They were brainwashed.

A holograph appeared in the center of the room, showing the hall moanitors speeding through the river of light on the Grim Reaper's ship. They were headed for Monster High. In Present's hand was the small glass box of boogie sand that would turn all the monsters into ghosts.

Spectra tried to control her panic. She had to stop this—but how?

A student hovering beside Spectra whispered, "No-good Solids! Trying to take over our school!"

"They never wanted to take over the school," she responded, furious. "I am sick of all of these rumors and gossip!"

She swooped out of the auditorium, determined to do something. Porter clanked after her. "Spectra! Where are you going?"

"I have to stop those hall moanitors!"

"How?"

"I have no idea!"

She flew through the main door, but Porter couldn't follow her. He slammed into the door and fell backward. His chains stopped him. Dazed, he began singing the jingle he'd written for their duo. "*Porter and Spectra! Crackin' the case! Something, something, something...*" He was too bleary to remember the words.

Spectra whizzed back through the door. She hadn't meant to leave Porter behind! "I'm so sorry! Your chains!"

But she couldn't abandon her classmates. She gave Porter a tiny kiss on the end of his hurt nose and dashed away again.

Slowly, Porter lifted his chain-covered arm and touched the end of his nose. He smiled. Spectra had kissed him!

While they were waiting for Spectra, Vandala was entertaining the ghosts with sea shanties played over her iCoffin. The skeleton pirates were dancing a jig when Spectra raced onboard, ordering them to set sail. "We have to go!" she urged.

Vandala looked longingly at the music.

"Now!" ordered Spectra.

"Aye aye!" agreed Vandala.

"Aye," echoed her cuttlefish.

Vandala took the wheel of the boat and eased it away from the dock. They were headed home. The ghouls crowded around Spectra, who had collapsed onto a bench.

"What's happening?" they asked her, concerned.

"It's Revenant," she explained. "She's sent the hall moanitors to Monster High to turn everyone into ghosts."

Twyla understood at once. "With my dad's boogie sand!"

Spectra nodded in agreement. "Then she wants to load them with detention chains! *Everybody!*" Spectra's eyes widened. That was it! At last she understood. "The chains! This is all about the detention chains!"

She paced back and forth along the deck. It was all beginning to make sense. "It's like Porter said. The chains can't be broken. Only transferred. Principal Revenant wasn't just wearing those chains," she said, remembering the principal with her long trail of clanking links, "she's being *punished* by them!"

Before her friends could respond, Spectra dove off the boat into the river below and began soaring toward Haunted High. "Do whatever you can to stop those hall moanitors," she called back to her friends.

Rochelle enviously watched her glide through the water. "No fair. How come she gets to go swimming?"

Porter hadn't left the main hall when Spectra reappeared. She zipped past him without stopping, even when he called after her. He struggled to follow her.

Spectra raced into the library, weaving in and out of the shelves. She was frantically searching for... something.

"Will you tell me what's going on?" begged Porter, staggering up to her.

Spectra grabbed a book and flipped through it. "Yes! This is it." She noticed Porter for the first time. "Come on. That desk you fixed is going to get some use after all." She handed Porter the mysterious book and vanished into his hidden studio.

Porter looked down at the book in his hands. It was all about the Red Lady!

CHAPTER 22

THE PRINCIPAL OF HAUNTINGS PAST

Rochelle leaned over the bow of the *Salty Specter*. "We are running out of time. Can you not make this thing go any faster, Vandala?"

"You heard the gargoyle!" Vandala shouted to her skeleton crew in the crow's nest. "Full speed ahead!"

One of the skeletons slid down the mast and began wheezing into the giant sails. Not that he had lungs… or breath. It didn't make a difference.

Vandala threw up her hands. "Looks like this *is* as fast as she goes," she said to Rochelle.

Twyla was worried. "We're going to be too late to stop the moanitors."

"Unless," Draculaura realized, looking at Kiyomi, "you could open a window! We'd get there in no time."

"Can you do it, Kiyomi?" asked River.

Kiyomi didn't answer. She was concentrating. Everyone waited. Would it work? A small yellow window appeared at the prow of the boat—and began opening!

"Fangtastic!" whooped Draculaura. "Let's move!"

Before stepping through the portal, Vandala removed her cuttlefish and gave him the steering wheel. "Aye, you're in charge while I'm away."

"Aye!" He saluted.

"Okay, now I'm ready!" said Vandala.

The ghouls tumbled through the window between the worlds—and burst out of Devlin's locker, sending the voodoo prince flying. They raced down the hallway of Monster High without even stopping to see if he was okay. As long as he wasn't a ghost yet—he was fine!

Clawdeen's brother, Clawd, and Deuce Gorgon were on their way to class when the ghosts flew past them, knocking them over and wailing like banshees. Terrified, the boys dove into the lockers, slamming them shut behind them. When the coast was clear, they peeked out. Clawd scratched his head. Was that Draculaura? He'd been wondering where she was...

In the main lobby, monsters were chatting with one

another and scribbling last-minute homework before the bell rang. Manny Taur didn't want to go to class. "Ugh." He sighed. "Another boring day at school..."

Before anyone could agree with him, the Grim Reaper's ghost ship descended through the ceiling and landed in the main lobby.

"I take it back." Manny gulped.

Principal Revenant watched the boat's arrival from the Haunted High auditorium. The ghosts were cheering. Present was loading the boogie sand into the confetti cannons!

"Time to boogie!" Past joked.

The moanitors laughed. Monsters were watching in amazement, trying to figure out what was going on. They had no idea they were in danger—until the ghouls flew into the lobby.

Sirena saw the cannon first.

"That is *not* the intended use for my confetti cannons!" River Styxx was mad.

"What are we gonna do?" asked Clawdeen. There was no time to lose.

Vandala took charge. "Let me show you ghouls a little something we learned in Ghost Pirating 101."

Present was getting ready to fire the cannon at the unsuspecting monsters when Vandala swung across the lobby on a ghost rope, waving her peg leg like a sword. "Yaaa-har ha harr!" As she swooped toward the deck, she reached out her hand and grabbed the box of boogie sand away from the cannon.

Watching on the projection at Haunted High, Principal Revenant was furious. "*No!* Stop those ghouls!"

As the rope swung back across the room, Vandala jumped down beside her friends, the precious box in her hands.

Rochelle was amazed. "Okay, now what?"

The moanitors were steering the ship straight toward them.

"Um." Vandala paused, catching her breath. "I think we run!"

"Right," agreed everyone.

They took off with the ship in close pursuit.

Back in the secret studio, Porter watched as Spectra typed at her computer. When he looked over her shoulder to see what she was writing, he was shocked. Could it really be true? This would explain *everything*. Spectra smiled at Porter. She'd figured it out.

Principal Revenant was blustering with rage in the auditorium. The ghouls had foiled her moanitors. Her plans were ruined. What else could possibly go wrong?

A voice came over the loudspeaker. It was Spectra. "*What I've Learned About Spreading Gossip.*

A *Haunted Herald* blog post by Spectra Vondergeist."

"What?" shrieked the principal. Her head swiveled around, and there was Spectra, holding her laptop on stage and reading what she'd written into a microphone. Porter was hovering beside her.

"Before coming to Haunted High," Spectra recounted, "I never saw much harm in reporting on rumors. They were just funny stories—little tidbits of juicy gossip. It was fun to join in with the crowd and pass along the latest overheard piece of news. But now I realize how harmful rumors can be—"

"Enough of this!" interrupted Principal Revenant.

But Spectra ignored her. "There's a particularly nasty rumor going around about how the so-called outsiders want to come to your school to frighten and scare you. It's not true—but this rumor became so powerful and so real that it was able to convince the entire school to go along with Principal Revenant's devious plan."

The real Principal Revenant, not the projection, sneered in her office. She'd show this troublemaker. All she needed was her key to bind her fast in chains—but where was it? It wasn't on her desk. With an impending sense of doom, she realized it was gone!

In the auditorium, Spectra continued. "And for what? Because she really thinks the Monster High students deserve detention? No. All this is because she wants to get rid of her *own* chains. And she has a lot of them. Because..." Spectra paused dramatically. Her audience was rapt. She cleared her throat. "Principal Revenant is the Red Lady!"

The students were stunned. There were whispers and gasps of shock.

"The Red Lady?"

"What is she talking about?"

"How can this be true?"

"It is true!" exclaimed Porter, stepping forward. "These are *her* chains!"

"This building," Spectra added, "it used to be her home. But her chains kept her from leaving, so she turned it into a school. The Red Lady wanted to give you all detention so that you could carry out her punishment for her."

"Look!"

"Up there!"

Students were pointing toward the ceiling where the real Principal Revenant was floating, her chains wafting around her like serpents. The key flew out of Porter's hand and landed in hers.

"That's quite enough blogging, Miss Vondergeist," she said snidely. "So you figured it out. I *am* the Red Lady. Good for you."

A red-hooded cloak materialized out of the ether

and draped itself over Principal Revenant. She lowered herself down to the stage so she could stare into Spectra's eyes. "Your little friends may have disrupted my plan, but it doesn't matter. If I can't have new students in detention, I'll just give all my chains to *you*!" Her key began to glow.

The ghost students were also watching the moanitors chase the ghosts through the halls of Monster High on the projection screen. Sirena was leading everyone toward the pool.

"They're too fast! We can't outrun them!" Twyla was almost out of breath.

"We have to keep going!" urged River Styxx.

But Kiyomi stopped in her tracks. She turned to face the oncoming ship. "No," she said bravely. "No more running."

"Kiyomi, what are you doing?" asked Draculaura, concerned.

Kiyomi sighed, resigned. "I started all of this by opening windows between worlds. Now I'm going to do the same to end it."

As the ship ploughed toward her, she tensed up, concentrating. A small yellow opening appeared. But it was just large enough for a single ghost to crawl through. Still, Kiyomi focused her energy. She was using all her psychic power to create a bigger portal.

"We have to help her!" said Draculaura.

"How?" asked River Styxx. "None of us has ever opened a window before."

Draculaura was not going to give up. "Group ghost power!"

The ghosts closed their eyes and began to concentrate. They imagined the window growing wider and wider—and slowly, very slowly, it began to open. An instant before the ship mowed them down, the portal widened all the way, and the boat sailed through it, back to the world of ghosts.

Long loops of chains were flying from Principal Revenant's body toward Spectra in the auditorium. The ghost braced for their impact. She was ready for them. One after another, they looped themselves around her—wrapping around her neck, her arms, her legs, her waist. More and more chains were flying through the air toward her. She could barely move— and still they were coming. How would she ever be free of this punishment?

Suddenly the ship burst into the auditorium at full speed, the moanitors at the helm. The boat headed right into the tangle of flying chains as it crashed. The ghouls at Monster High entered as well, closing the portal behind them.

"That'll teach you to mess with another reaper's confetti cannons!" shouted River Styxx triumphantly.

Draculaura patted Kiyomi on the back. "Nice shot!"

But Principal Revenant didn't care. Nothing mattered now that she was free of her chains—they were all wrapped around Spectra. With a sweeping wave of her hands, she opened another portal to the Monster World. "It's been fun, boys and ghouls, it really has. But if you'll excuse me, I've got a lot of haunting to catch up on…"

She cackled wickedly and rose up to the window, but when she tried to pass through, she was slammed backward with an explosive burst of yellow energy. She banged on the window with her fists. It was as solid as a wall. "No! No! Why can't I leave? I don't have any more chains!"

But she did.

A single glowing detention chain was twining around her ankle.

"What's happening?" Principal Revenant panicked. "Who's doing this?" Her eyes fell on Spectra. "Is it you? Or is it your little ghoulfriends?" She shook her fist. *"Who is doing this to me?"*

Spectra understood at last. "You're doing it to yourself," she revealed.

A glimmer of understanding blanched the principal's face. "No." She shuddered.

"See for yourself," said Spectra. "The chains are coming from you."

Principal Revenant looked in horror as another chain wrapped itself around her leg.

"It all makes sense," continued Spectra. "Look around at your students. All those chains you've given out, and yet you weren't getting any closer to freedom. Because with every haunting, every unjustified detention, every lie, every rumor, and every bit of gossip that you spread—you were creating more chains for yourself."

Principal Revenant didn't want to admit that it was true. "Somebody else must be doing this!"

"No," said Spectra. "Deep down, I think you knew what you were doing was wrong. And your inner conscience created these chains to try and stop you. You said it yourself—you'll never learn your lesson if you don't pay the price." She turned to the assembled students. They had to know the truth. "The Solids are not out to get you. They're just like you and me. That was all just made-up ghost gossip. I don't know about you, but I am done with rumors."

Clawdeen grinned at Spectra. "Good for you, ghoulfriend. Told you we'd find you a good story."

Principal Revenant knew she'd been beaten. She was downcast but determined. She still had her key. It was time to make amends. "I spent so much time blaming everyone else that I never stopped to consider that this was…my fault."

She pressed the key, and all the students' chains lit up. They broke apart, then flew into the air toward Principal Revenant. Spectra was free. Porter was free. Everyone was free.

There were jubilant cheers from the crowd.

"No more detention!"

"Thank you, Principal Revenant!"

Principal Revenant was covered in more chains than ever before, but she seemed to accept her fate—for the first time. "I'm sorry I made you all a part of this. These are my chains to work off. Not yours. No matter how long it takes. I hope you'll let me continue being your principal while I pay for my mistakes." The key levitated out of her hands. It burst into smithereens—leaving nothing but pale yellow dust.

The students applauded.

Principal Revenant looked down at her ankle. A single link on one of her chains had disappeared. This was the only way to make them vanish—by doing good deeds. "I'll earn my freedom. Someday," she said. She already seemed nicer.

Spectra flew over to Porter

"Can I just say—that was totally spooktacular," he complimented her.

Spectra blushed. "You thought so?"

"I had chills," he admitted. "And not just because, you know, I'm a ghost."

Students crowded around them, everyone wanting to know if it was true about the outsiders.

Spectra looked at Porter. She had an idea. A *very* good idea. "I think it's about time these two schools got to know each other!"

CHAPTER 23

GHOST HOSTS

BOOM! BOOM! BOOM!

The confetti cannons announced a Monster High–Haunted High party on the ship! Ghosts and monsters were mingling, music was blaring from the ship's speakers, and a glowing yellow window was open, connecting the two schools. Principal Revenant was carrying around a tray of refreshments and every time she smiled, another link disappeared.

Porter's pet raccoon was painting a mural—featuring River's raven, Vandala's cuttlefish, Kiyomi's Kaiju, and himself. Vandala was swinging from the balcony on a rope. "Yaaar!" she yelled as she flew over the crowd.

She landed on the deck in front of Frankie, Cleo, and Ghoulia. "Okay, now you try." She laughed.

"Yar!" said Frankie in her sweet voice.

"Yar?" tried Cleo.

Ghoulia moaned.

"We'll work on it." Vandala laughed.

Toralei and the werecats walked by. They were scratching their arms and their ears. "Ugh," whined Toralei. "Why am I so itchy all of a sudden?"

Vandala looked at the red marks on Toralei. "I've seen this before. You've got sea-fleas."

Toralei freaked out. "Sea-fleas!!!!"

On the other side of the ship, Rochelle, Sirena, and Lagoona were diving into the pool. Rochelle, still a ghost, was having a blast flipping effortlessly through the water. Johnny, Operetta, and Scarah were lounging in chairs on the deck.

Clawd and Manny were teaching a crew of ghosts how to play Casketball. Clawd was spinning a ball on his finger. "I think our schools should play sometime."

"Yeah, dude," agreed Deuce.

BOOM! BOOM! BOOM!

Twyla was setting off the confetti cannons while River, in her reaper hood, was spinning the turntable. The hall moanitors were swabbing the deck, but they seemed a lot happier now that they weren't giving out chains.

Kiyomi was styling Draculaura's hair. "There!" she said. "All finished." It was even prettier than when she had hauntingly styled it without Draculaura knowing.

"Spooky chic!" exclaimed River Styxx.

Spectra and Porter drifted away from the crowd to the top of the ship. Clawdeen joined them. "So rumor has it that the ghosts and the monsters are really hitting it off."

Porter grinned. "Hey, I think I read a blog post that said there's nothing good about spreading rumors."

"I think this one is okay." Clawdeen laughed. She wandered away, leaving the ghosts alone.

"You know," said Porter when she was gone. "I'm really gonna miss seeing you at school every day."

Spectra smiled. She took Porter's hand in hers. "I'm really gonna miss you too, Porter, but you know what?" She gazed into his eyes. "I'll just be a boat ride away."

The music grew louder, the cuttlefish started dancing, and the ghosts and the monsters celebrated their first ever dual-school party—but certainly not their last!

CHAPTER 24

MOANITOR MADNESS

Later that night as she was getting into bed, Twyla heard shuffling in the boogie mansion. She could swear someone was in the house. It sounded like he or she was headed to her father's study. Quietly, she headed into the hall. Now she was sure she heard the thumping backbeat of a bass. Someone was playing music!

"Huh?" she wondered, tiptoeing toward the study.

She flung open the door to surprise whomever was there, and then flicked on the light.

It was the hall moanitors! They were playing with the boogie sand!

Past was a yeti, Present was a pig monster, and Future was a duck vampire.

They froze mid–dance step. Busted!

Twyla just shook her head. The last thing she was going to do tonight was spoil *anyone*'s fun.

The moanitors looked at one another after she left. They waited. They giggled. And they started dancing again! It was time to boogie!